THE MISPLACED PSYCHE

THE MISPLACED PSYCHE

Lauran Paine

Chivers Press • G.K. Hall & Co.
Bath, England • Thorndike, Maine USA

This Large Print edition is published by Chivers Press, England, and by G.K. Hall & Co., USA.

Published in 1997 in the U.K. by arrangement with Robert Hale Limited.

Published in 1997 in the U.S. by arrangement with Golden West Literary Agency.

U.K. Hardcover ISBN 0–7451–6955–4 (Chivers Large Print)
U.S. Softcover   ISBN 0–7838–1970–6 (Nightingale Collection Edition)

Copyright © 1973 by Lauran Paine
Copyright © 1997 by Lauran Paine

The text of this Large Print edition is unabridged.
Other aspects of the book may vary from the original edition.

Set in 16 pt. New Times Roman.

Printed in Great Britain on acid-free paper.

British Library Cataloguing in Publication Data available

Library of Congress Cataloging-in-Publication Data

Paine, Lauran.
   The misplaced psyche / Lauran Paine.
      p.   cm.
   ISBN 0–7838–1970–6 (lg. print : sc)
   1. Large type books.   I. Title.
[PS3566.A34M5   1997]
813'.54—dc20   96–30932

CONTENTS

CONTENTS

CHAPTER ONE

DOCTOR WALTER WHALEN

What prompted Doctor Whalen's endeavour was the fact that the administration of anaesthesia almost without exception produced some degree of adverse effect upon post-operative patients.

In cases where undetectable allergic reaction occurred, it was not uncommon for the patient to have a harder time recovering from the anaesthesia than from the surgery.

Even in normal cases physical tolerance to the various anaesthetics was very rarely what could have been wished. As Doctor Whalen had said a number of times, anaesthetics were not only relatively new, but while their variety was great, they were still basically created around a chemical drug of one kind or another that was powerful enough to stun and overwhelm and upset the normal physical-bental awareness, and anything like that, but particularly the crude concoctions currently in use in every hospital in the world, ranging all the way from mixtures containing addictive drugs to paralysing agents, was bound to leave post-operative patients deathly ill just as a result of the anaesthetic, leaving their surgery out of it altogether.

1

Doctor Whalen was not an anaesthesiologist. His speciality was angiology, which made him qualified in the field of veins and arteries, the field of atherosclerosis, circulation and so forth, and what originally caused his critical view of anaesthetics was the number of open-heart cases he had collaborated in. He was not a surgeon so he did none of the actual internal work, but Doctor Whalen *was* a highly intelligent, essentially critical, lifelong anthropologist along with being thoroughly qualified in his particular field. Therefore, and since heart surgery was the most delicate variety of all, even more delicate than brain surgery, when Doctor Whalen had to watch his post-operative patients struggling to live after the surgery, and at the same time suffering intensely from the after-effects of an anaesthetic, being the kind of outspoken man he was, Doctor Whalen not only denounced current anaesthetics, he spent three years seeking an alternative, and he succeeded in finding one.

But the hospital with which he was affiliated—for a time anyway—would not be convinced of the need for any procedure that was a radical departure from traditional practice, and its Chief Resident absolutely refused, and rightly perhaps, to allow Doctor Whalen's discovery to be tried. His animadversion was clinical not personal. He

2

was a friend of long-standing of Walter Whalen.

'You know perfectly well that we're not in the guinea-pig business,' he told Doctor Whalen. 'The place for experimentation is in the laboratory, not a community hospital.'

Whalen's rebuttal was equally as valid. 'I have perfected the technique on animals, John, and it works exactly as I've explained to you. But somewhere along the line, since the entire idea was developed to help *people*, I have to try it on a human being.'

'Not here, you don't, and that is final.'

John Ames was one of the most respected surgeons in America. His credentials were recognised world-wide. He was also an accomplished administrator, otherwise he never would have been Chief Resident at Boston General Hospital. He had taken his medical degree in London, had practised in Britain and Canada before settling at Boston General, in Massachusetts. He was a tall, erect, incisive Englishman, and thirty years after leaving England, although he had changed in many ways, had become Americanised in speech and largely in outlook, he was still possessed of the most notable English characteristic: stubbornness. He and Walter Whalen played golf together, dined together—they were both bachelors—and co-operated closely and very well at Boston General, but every time Doctor Whalen brought up his

3

innovation Doctor Ames reacted in the same way.

'No! Not here!'

What annoyed Walter Whalen about this undeviating and uncompromising rejection was that, not only did he have no other source of ill people to try his innovation upon, but, as he had explained to Doctor Ames at least a dozen times, there really was no danger.

'I will undertake the accomplishment with you and all the other members of staff in attendance,' he told John Ames. 'There is no administration of medicine, so you won't have to worry about what I'm shooting into someone. The entire idea is founded upon an ability to divorce patients about to undergo surgery from physical consciousness. Instead of drugging them with some damned variety of ether or chloroform or some addictive concoction derived from opium or the like, my system simply removes their etheric awareness entirely, and after surgery when they are brought back, so to speak, there are no side-effects nor after-effects; no headaches, no vomiting, no possibility of physical allergic reaction at all.'

Doctor Ames had an answer. 'You're beginning to sound like a hypnotist, Walter, and you should know as well as anyone else that hypnotism may help in childbirth and in other matters that are more or less natural physical functions, but it simply will not do in

4

cases of major surgery.'

'I am *not* talking about hypnotism,' exclaimed Whalen. 'I'm not even suggesting putting the consciousness to sleep, or trying to influence it to blank out the concepts of pain. What I've tried to get across to you, John, is that instead of having patients sick as dogs with mile-high hangovers from anaesthetics after surgery, there is a way to simply divorce them from what is happening to them in such a way that they will feel absolutely nothing— nothing at all—because their consciousness will be separated from their bodies until the surgery is completed, then it is put back as gently as awakening from a pleasant sleep, and there are no bad after-effects because there have been no anaesthetics administered.'

Doctor Ames gave the same answer: 'Not here!'

For Walter Whalen defeat was synonymous with death. He had been a medical practitioner too long, and had scrimped and struggled and fought too long to become one, to accept any other kind of defeat. His lifelong conviction had been that as long as there was breath, there was hope. He did not abandon his compulsion to test the innovation upon a patient, but finding one to test it upon was another matter. He had a large, and lucrative, practice. It took all his time, but even if this had not been true, Doctor Whalen was not in a position to go out and find some indigent who might, for enough

5

money, allow himself to be experimented upon. Also, there was the matter of ethics. If some such volunteer were to be found, there were laws against medical practitioners conducting private experiments on people; those laws were unwritten as well as written. Even if everything turned out precisely as Doctor Whalen knew it would, more than one medical association would strongly question Walter Whalen's ethics.

There was one way: take a sabbatical, perhaps a year or so, form an affiliation with an experimentation laboratory, and do the work there. The disadvantages were twofold: He would probably lose his position at Boston General. There were lists of doctors waiting to get on with John Ames's establishment. The second disadvantage was that Walter Whalen would lose his income for as long as the sabbatical endured, a year more or less, and that was a very painful prospect. Walter Whalen was accustomed to living on sixty-five thousand dollars annually. He was not a spend-thrift, but the idea of living off savings, perhaps having to liquidate some real estate holdings, some stocks and bonds, was very distasteful. Moreover, it was also very exasperating, because he knew in his heart the innovation did not require all that sacrifice to be proven.

In a way, it was like standing with Christopher Columbus on the bow of his ship knowing without a solitary doubt what lay beyond the misty horizon, and being circumvented, harassed, scorned and ridiculed by everyone. Columbus persevered, and so would Walter Whalen. Of course Columbus afterwards suffered even worse dehumanisation, and died in penury and disgrace.

There was one ameliorating circumstance; Doctor Whalen's work. When he was not involved at Boston General he saw private patients in a handsome suite of offices where a secretary and a nurse managed his appointments and his professional life very smoothly, very efficiently.

There had been a tendency on the part of the private practice to grow beyond Walter Whalen's wishes. He wanted to be busy, true, but he did *not* want to be overwhelmed. His years of near-hunger putting himself through medical school after college, and the subsequent internships which had paid barely enough to keep body and soul together, were behind him now. What he proposed doing with the remainder of his life was much less grim and strenuous. He wanted to practice, but he also wanted to *live*. In fact, that was the main reason why he took the offer when it was made by John Ames, to become a consultant on the staff at Boston General.

His clientele was by no means run-of-the-mill. That was the main advantage in

7

specialising in an area where the income-level was above the national norm. Even Walter Whalen's poorer patients were better-heeled than the average among patients in other cities. Boston was a financial centre, an area of accrued as well as inherited wealth, and Doctor Whalen's speciality was in a field that was related to the debilities arising from hypertension as well as age. Financiers, money-men of all kinds, were notoriously prone to circulatory ailments; heart attacks, hardening of the arteries, occlusions, angustations. Doctor Whalen had his share of these types. He had, in fact, become socially affiliated with several men whose advice on matters of investment Doctor Whalen had followed, to his benefit. Otherwise, his private practice, while not large, was adequate to keep him occupied, and if he had decided to sever relations with Boston General, he could easily have doubled the private practice. But he did not want to do that. Boston General Hospital was a fascinating large, very modern, very challenging and enlightening place. He enjoyed the society of the other practitioners and his friendship with John Ames went back to their years of internship at the same institution.

Taken all together, Walter Whalen's life had been, up to the time of his attempt to improve upon anaesthesia, exactly as he had wished to order it. It had been rewarding in every meaning of that noun, satisfactory in the social sense, and financially compensatory. Except for his desire to improve upon the traditional and primitive science of anaesthesia, there was no reason at all for Walter Whalen not to predict the flow of his life from that point until he ultimately retired a wealthy man with extensive and diversified holdings.

That was what the practice of medicine was all about, in America, and not only in America but everywhere else that practitioners prognosticated, except that in the more enlightened countries doctors were not allowed to bankrupt the ill and ailing in order to pile up great fortunes. That was strictly an American phenomenon.

CHAPTER TWO

ROUTINES AND A PATIENT

Three years was a long time to innovate; a long time to spend perfecting something from theory to fact, only to have it summarily rejected when the innovator knew as well as he knew his own name that it was not some kind of crack-pot creation.

Walter Whalen had tried his innovation upon rats and mice at first, then had gone on to try it on dogs, cats, two Rhesus monkeys, a

9

series of birds, and on a horse. In every instance it had worked perfectly.

He had subjected the experimental animals to pain, mild initially, then more intense, and finally to excruciating varieties of pain. Not a single animal had felt anything. Afterwards, they had healed normally and immediately following the experiment when they would normally have evinced the post-operative slump due to anaesthetic drugs they showed very clearly that no such reaction obtained.

The final year of his lab work Walter Whalen did very little to improve or alter the innovation itself, which was based upon electronic principles, he had instead perfected the administering techniques, and he had experimented time and time again, sacrificing his Saturdays and Sundays and a great many of his afternoons and evenings, when this had been possible.

The innovation was very simple, both in the way he created it, and in principle. In the same way that a soundless dog whistle created a noise pitched too high for human ears, Walter Whalen's innovation could be plugged into any electrical wall-outlet for current, and when activated it could then be made, by means of a magnetic rheostat, to suffuse the brain with decibels of soundlessness that simply lifted out the consciousness.

On every animal, this limboed consciousness had remained separate from the brain for as

10

long as the suffusion lasted, and that was for as long as Doctor Whalen left the plug in the electrical wall-outlet, or for as long as he kept the rheostat turned to its highest pitch.

To re-settle the consciousness, Walter Whalen had, in his first few experiments, simply pulled the plug, but later he perfected the technique of turning the rheostat down very gradually by hand, allowing the consciousness to settle-in more gently. This latter method was the one he used in all the later experiments. By the time he was completely satisfied, he was good enough with the innovation that he could bring an animal around to normalcy in about two minutes, and without a single noticeable after-effect to the suffusion. There was no nausea, no headache, no listlessness, no side-effects of any kind whatsoever.

There was also no reason to believe that the Whalen Innovation was not the break-through anaesthesiology had been waiting in order to keep pace with the vast advances being made in just about every other field of medicine and the healing arts. Except that Walter Whalen could not convince John Ames it was worth trying.

Doctor Whalen, being an unattached man with almost no interest in women, the result of not having been able to afford that interest when he had been young enough to strongly feel it, spent many of his nights in the expensively equipped and sophisticated

11

laboratory he had created in the back of his costly residence. Occasionally he went out to supper, or to a theatre, or to a party. He was neither a recluse nor a complete misogynist. On the other hand he had disciplined himself over the years to believe in his profession above everything else. Therefore, when he thought he had the secret, the answer to current methods of rendering the luckless unconscious during surgery, he dedicated himself almost exclusively, during the free hours to his creation, and when it was perfected beyond any shadow of a doubt, his exasperation was very deep and very abiding.

But he had little time to brood, even if he had been the kind of man who brooded, which he was not, although it could have been said that in appearance at any rate, he resembled the kind of a man who might be inward.

Walter Whalen was about average in height, maybe an inch less than average. He had dark hair and dark eyes. He was a stocky, perfectly-co-ordinated, physically compact and muscular man whose paternal grandfather, whom he resembled, had emigrated to America from Wales slightly more than a hundred years earlier.

That same grandfather had died a coal miner. Doctor Whalen's father had followed the same vocation, and had also died a coal miner, but at an age which was early even for coal miners—forty-three—and that had been

12

the start of Doctor Whalen's interest in medicine; it could be said that his father's early passing was also Doctor Whalen's medical-profession motivation. And if John Ames had the English characteristic of stubbornness, Walter Whalen certainly possessed an equally as characteristic Welsh affinity for the same vice—or virtue.

Even when he finally became quite convinced he would not be able to demonstrate his innovation at Boston General Hospital, Doctor Whalen persevered. Less in his experiments, because after a year of almost monotonous success that was no longer necessary, but in trying to devise some way to demonstrate the break-through he had fathered.

He purposefully cultivated three other Chief Residents and over a period of months enticed each one of them to agree with him that current anaesthesiology was archaic. Then he explained his theory and his practical application, and in both instances met the same dogmatic, but friendly, denunciation he had got from Doctor Ames.

After that, for half a year, he devoted himself to his speciality. He had not given up, but for the time being he could not imagine another avenue to explore, and anyway, during this particular time he was very busy.

Boston General's intensive care unit seldom was without a coronary patient, and most of

13

the time it had several, as many in fact as twenty or thirty at a time. This seemed usually to coincide with the holidays, and it was generally thought such a condition obtained because it was particularly during November and December that people ate and drank and overdid just about everything a little more than they normally did any other time of the year.

Some of the cardiac patients were prominent; in fact, a few of them were *very* prominent, either in the financial or the political context. As Doctor Ames smilingly told Walter Whalen in a glistening corridor one day, 'It wouldn't surprise me a bit if we got the Vice-President up from Washington one of these days. Boston General's getting quite a reputation. Incidentally, there's a new one on the way, Walter. Charles Southcott, the international investment banker. Do look in on him as soon as he arrives, won't you?'

Walter Whalen 'looked-in' on all of them as a matter of hospital procedure, so Ames's injunction really hadn't been necessary, except as a reminder, or perhaps as a warning, that *this* patient was someone special.

Whalen was not especially impressed. He knew who Charles Southcott was because he read the *Wall Street Journal*, among other financial publications, but he could have been the Rajah of Mysore or the Chairman of the Supreme Soviet and he would still have been

14

de-dignified the moment he became ill enough to enter the spacious receiving lobby of Boston General. Doctor Whalen had seen them all, at one time or another, during his association with the hospital, and even if he hadn't, his professional attitude was soundly based upon an interest in ailing flesh, without particular regard to whose ailing flesh it was.

He was in the staff's consultation room drinking coffee and looking out into the bleak, late November day when Charles Southcott arrived. Beyond the sealed window naked trees writhed under the whiplash of a gusty wind, and the little patch of grass nearby was as brown and dead as it could be.

There was a storm overhead, either passing through or, if the wind abated, pausing directly above the city. Boston, in summertime, was a pretty place; too big and ugly in its extremities, like all cities, and too soiled as well, but when the sun shone Boston's parks and suburbs were handsome. There were a lot worse cities. Even the small one in the West Virginia coalfields where Walter Whalen had been born, and had grown to stocky young manhood, was uglier and more depressing, although it was usually claimed that rural villages were pretty; were at least hectic and ugly, than places like Boston, Massachusetts.

The intercom called Doctor Whalen in muted tones. He finished the coffee and left the room. The stormy, depressing day outside

15

could not reach him as soon as he left the window. Boston General was a large, solid, self-sufficient, self-contained antiseptic world. Its routines were established; had been established and perfected through generations of trial and error. The personnel of Boston General did not make mistakes. At least not in the categories that included section heads, physicians, surgeons, and administrators. Occasionally lesser people erred, but one powerful advantage of the medical profession was that its fellows did not err. There was one basic flaw in the medical profession, but there was a circumstance that ameliorated it, thus doctors could say without undue worry of contradiction, that each prognosis was correct.

The flaw was simply that a medical education could instill in a person a vast amount of priceless knowledge, but neither that sophisticated education nor that great knowledge could ever become a substitute for the lack of good judgement heredity had deprived a person of. Not all doctors came from the kind of human stock that possessed sound judgement. A doctor could graduate in medicine, for example, but a heritage of a thousand years of Balkan peasantry behind him would never qualify him to possess the wisdom, the judgement, the advantage of genuine intellect good medical practice required.

The amelioration, on the other hand, was

simply that when someone like Charles Southcott arrived at a hospital, he was already in an ailing condition, and anything at all that was done to improve either his condition or his comfort, would make him feel better than he had felt before his arrival.

When Doctor Whalen first entered Southcott's private room this was the thought in his mind. Charles Southcott was a very sick man. It required no tests to see that this was so. Just the general routine was going to help him, so whether he could respond to anything else, or not, he would be improved by being there.

Southcott was not as old as Whalen had imagined he would be. In fact, Whalen and Charles Southcott were the same age, forty-four, although Whalen did not know it when he was introducing himself to the ailing financier and his overly-cultured, mink-draped wife.

Whalen was quiet and calm and brisk. There would be tests for the balance of this day, and the results should be available by tomorrow. Otherwise, it was advisable if Mrs Southcott left, and did not return this evening, as was customary, but would visit her husband perhaps the following afternoon. Generally, it was Whalen's practice to prescribe sleep and relaxation, as much of both for the patient as he could get. There were two reasons for this: one was because everyone arriving at a hospital was anxious and worried and depressed. The other reason was because until the results of the tests were known, there really was nothing Walter Whalen could discuss with Charles Southcott.

Southcott was a thick-necked, burly man, resembling a longshoreman more than a financier. He had the pursed lips, the blue-ice kind of probing eyes, and the general appearance of a man who listened only to his own drummer. He did not, now, quite exude the kind of strong confidence his kind of a man normally evinced, but then very few people, successful or not successful, ever entered a hospital feeling as they felt outside in their familiar and predictable world.

Southcott was a handsome man, beginning to grey at the temples, still fairly athletic-looking. He could smile and when his wife was no longer present, his language was salted with healthy profanity.

Walter Whalen liked him. Whalen was not a pretentious person and evidently neither was Charles Southcott, the financial wizard.

What kind of a patient Southcott would be was another matter. Doctor Whalen had seen many of Southcott's type, and as a rule they were not good patients; at least they were not *docile* patients.

But time would tell about that.

When Doctor Whalen departed to give orders for the tests he wanted Southcott to have, he had already made a tentative

18

diagnosis: Charles Southcott, a hypertension-type, was a week, maybe a month, away from a coronary.

Of course it could happen this afternoon, but the odds were against that, and after all the analyses were in, Doctor Whalen would know more. So would Charles Southcott, because Doctor Whalen would tell him.

CHAPTER THREE

CHARLES SOUTHCOTT

A healthy man is immortal. He can't die, he can't even actually convince himself illness can touch him, and if he is strong-willed and successful, those possibilities are even more remote, providing he is active and busy.

Until the crisis arrives.

For Charles Southcott the little twinges of pain had been noticeable and negligible; something a human being learned to live with. From his football days in college to his present forty-fourth year, because he had always been a participant, no matter what the sport was, there had been sprains, bruises, pain of one kind or another. He had survived them all and had steamrollered his way to the top. He had the drive, the fiercely competitive will, to achieve, to emerge on top.

19

He had always done this and he always would try to do it. And someday, in the distant future, he would go to bed surrounded by a family—except that he had none, no children anyway, just a horde of ingratiating in-laws—and quietly die.

Something like that, at any rate. It had to happen, when a man was full of years, but a man of forty-four was hardly full of years.

The little twinges got more frequent and one afternoon at the club, in the handball court right after a hard-fought game—he had won—there had been a moment of breathlessness, a kind of strange nausea accompanied by a slight dizziness. The club physician had suggested a complete physical examination. Charles Southcott had flown out of Boston International Airport the following day for London on business. Over there, he had another of those sensations, only this time the nausea had hung on. An English physician, with impersonal detachment had said, 'You have a bad heart, Mister Southcott. You can of course go right on as you have been doing, and sooner or later it'll stop, and that will take care of everything very abruptly, probably. Or you can go into hospital when you get back home, and perhaps live for many years.'

And now he was lying in a room with a bad watercolour on one wall, watching a storm building beyond his private window, and the pain in his chest, which had become almost a daily routine now, was less than it had been in months.

If the sun had been shining, if the trees had had leaves, if the sky had been less leaden and forbidding and there had been grass and birds outside, he knew for a fact that his mood would have been different. But he was lying there, waiting for the damned tests to be made, looking out into the wintry face of death, and that changed everything. He was *not* immortal, and that was harder to accept, even, than the possibility of sudden death.

Margaret.

Margaret had had the longest legs and the most beautiful suntan of any girl, during Charles Southcott's last year at college. She had also turned out to have the most violently possessive and demanding physical passion.

That was almost twenty years ago. *That* Margaret had died somewhere, back during the tough years of struggle. The present Margaret Morton Southcott, with the handsome figure, the classically perfect face, and the cold hauteur that kept increasing as the millions had piled up, was a stranger.

Charles Southcott would not have married *this* Margaret if she'd consumed him with passion, back in those earlier days. *This* Margaret was exactly the type of woman he had despised in college; the daughters of millionaires who had turned his stomach, and that was ironic. *That* Margaret had turned into

21

precisely what he had detested in women all his life.

As for the money—what the hell good was it to a dead man? He probably would not die; not this time. People who had coronary seizures in hospitals did not die as a general rule. But a man with a thousand details mixed up in his life, all of them having to do with a cumulative kind of wealth, could not spend his whole gawddamned life in a hospital, either.

Some day the damned heart would get him. Once he faced that fact it was easier to live with the destroyed image of mortality. He even felt a kind of defiant, fatalistic humour. The healthiest, strongest, most indestructible man in college, and later in the hard years, and right up until now, was turning out to have feet of clay. That was funny. It did not make him want to laugh out loud, but nevertheless it was funny.

A man lived his life by the established rules, and this is where it got him. In an ugly little plain room with a bad watercolour on the wall, while his sprawling hundred-thousand-dollar suburban mansion with its quarter of a million dollars worth of furnishings, was standing out there miles away as though it, and not he, were the important thing.

Margaret's mausoleum, he had often called it—to himself. Margaret's gawddamned monument to *her*—not *his*—success. The pastel walls, the subdued servants, the carpets

22

that you could lose a shoe in, the original oils that looked like a madman had drawn their abstract squares and zig-zags. The deferential people Margaret invited in at least once a week to share candlelight suppers with the silver polished and displayed so she, and the damned sterling, could hold court.

He had considered divorce a dozen times, and each time he had ended up doing the same thing; hurling himself into his work, and that was ironic because he had then accumulated more wealth, and she had used it to enrichen her damned mausoleum to impress more ingratiating people. The vicious circle.

She had definitely ruled out a family long ago. Women with children lost their figures, were not free to travel, and children spoiled furniture and ruined landscape grounds.

Charles Southcott came back from his reverie when the nurses arrived, along with some kind of white-coated technologist who had what resembled a large radio mounted on a wheeled stand. This machine had electrodes sticking out of it like an array of spider-legs. The young man said something about cardiology, about computerised tests that would be transmitted to New York City where an almost instantaneous diagnosis would be made, and he said it all as though Charles Southcott should be very impressed.

He was not impressed. What the hell difference did it make whether they found out his heart was leaking, or something, within fifteen minutes from distant New York City, if they did not know how to make a lousy heart whole and strong again?

He lay inertly and allowed them to attach the electrodes. Twenty-eight million dollars, still a young man, one of the most admired—by clothiers anyway—wives on the East Coast, success in every direction like a golden sunray—and here he lay like an oversized hog waiting for a thin youth with thick glasses and a white, belt-length coat to decide whether he was going on, or whether he was not going on.

All the things a man dedicated his entire lifetime to, all the solid and substantial things that really mattered—did not matter at all!

What he really wanted right now was a double scotch and soda, and after that a rich Sumatran cigar.

One of the nurses had very bright blue eyes and a full, sweet mouth. She had to be no more than twenty-five years old. She also had a wedding band. Charles Southcott had a sudden wistful longing, and closed his eyes.

The young man began peeling off the electrodes. As he did this he said, 'We will have the results for your physician very shortly,' and Charles Southcott, speaking from the depth of his shattered immortality, and without opening his eyes, said, 'I don't have a doctor. Now get the hell out of here.'

They got. The technician went in search of

Walter Whalen with a scrap of information that was not really very surprising. 'Doctor, that Charles Southcott is just exactly what you would expect him to be. Discourteous and blunt. I'll work up the results of the test and get them to you in a little while.'

Charles Southcott was, in fact, blunt. His people preferred to call it 'forthright,' but not everyone was that charitable. But he was seldom discourteous; not knowingly so. There was a disparity—there *had* to be one—between Charles Southcott and every normal, ambulatory human being living through an average day. In hospital it might have been expected that this would be understood. It wasn't. That technician, those nurses, were not intelligent people, just *trained* people. There was an obvious difference.

Charles Southcott was sure he would never have another average day. He had arrived at that conclusion after listening to the physician in London: if he avoided a coronary, if the hospital in Boston could alleviate, if it could not correct his difficulty, he might live several more years. He might even live a considerable number of years. And then again he might never leave this damned bed.

There was no way for him to have a normal, average, day again, as long as he lived.

A lot of things took a lot of getting accustomed to. Values of long standing had to be re-assessed and shuffled to make room for

25

newer and different values. The things Charles Southcott believed in, the things he had rarely ever thought about, and the things, like death, which he had never considered at all, at least not properly, had to be re-arranged in the scale of values according to fresh priorities.

This entire episode was a shock and a revelation. By evening, when he was finally beginning to accept the only philosophy available to him, peace came, although resignation eluded him. That would arrive later, when the stocky doctor came in and sat down like a teacher in nursery school and explained things.

Patience came, which was akin to resignation, and as he lay looking out into the wind scourged stormy dusk, the antithesis crossed his mind, then lingered.

Three years ago, about this same time of year, he had been in France on business, and it had been as bitter and bleak as Massachusetts in November. It had looked, in fact, not at all different out his hotel window, than it looked now, out the hospital window. Then he had taken a tip from a Frenchman. 'Go to Barcelona this time of year. Enjoy a little sunshine before going back to New England.'

He had gone. He had deserved a day or two of diversion. Anyway, when a man goes everywhere by jet airplane, there really is no off-course place, not when nothing more than an hour or two of flight time is involved.

And now he remembered, lying in his hospital bed. Not Barcelona especially, although it lay in blessed sunwash between the Gulf of Lions and the Balearics, facing the greeny-grey Mediterranean, a great, noisy, alien place. What he remembered was the Catalonian village on the north side of the Ebros.

If that village had a name he did not remember it, but everything else came back. He remembered standing there and looking, and feeling different than he had ever felt in other villages. The weight of time lay everywhere, and although he came from a nation not yet even two hundred years old, he had nevertheless visited ancient towns in other parts of the world, so it had to be something else that held him there in hot sunlight standing beside the rented car, looking and watching-- and feeling—this different place.

There were goats, some sheep as well, mountains like crumpled brown and green cartons, north, south, and east. Westerly lay the gradual slope of the old and eroded soil towards the sea.

There was fruit, of course, and olives, and a rippling quicksilver lift and fall of foreign voices, and dust everywhere that stirred like old gold when men and women and children crossed through it.

There were girls who seemed more Basque than Catalonian which was entirely possible.

There were little boys with hair so black it shone blue, and little girls with eyes that were both very young, and very old.

The men were quiet but willing; they sought only respect, without once asking for it. They were sinewy, hardy and belonged nowhere on earth except where Charles Southcott saw them.

The women seemed either to be young or old. If there were middle-aged women, he did not see them that day. He did not really know about gypsies, but he saw long-legged girls in that village, supple and exquisite with dark whites to their eyes, and thought of gypsies.

And one he saw, the girl and her man, coming down from the direction of an ancient church hand in hand, he sombre to the point of sad gloominess, and she with a sweet hopefulness that made her face beautiful in the soft fading afternoon.

He remembered that face, that expression, as clearly as though instead of having seen it three years ago, he had seen it yesterday. He remembered, too, the pain in his chest that afternoon, but it was a different pain. He remembered that young man with pleasant envy, and he remembered the girl with the variety of wistfulness all men who have lost love, feel, when they see it once again.

CHAPTER FOUR

SOME CONVENIENT CIRCUMSTANCES

Historically, in great and small matters, there have never been but two approaches to a revelation, the tactful and the forthright, and while Walter Whaler had learned tact, he was not by nature a tactful person. Nor did he believe Charles Southcott was tactful, either, or likely to appreciate tact in relation to his present condition.

But Doctor Whalen, who had been associating with ill people for many years and understood the psychology of illness, waited. He had the cardiology reports the afternoon of Southcott's admission to Boston General, so he could have gone down the hall to Southcott's room, with plenty of time to spare, on his daily exit from the hospital. Instead, he read the report, analysed it soberly, reduced it to words that had relevance to non-medical people, then went home.

The following morning he waited until about ten o'clock. Southcott had been fed, had bathed and shaved, and was lying there beginning to feel impatience instead of the previous day's depression, when Doctor Whalen arrived, took a chair, and began his cryptic explanation. Charles Southcott

29

required heart surgery. There was no guarantee he would be as good as new, afterwards, but the variety of operation he needed was fairly routine. It was being done every day, in some hospital in America. Basically, the need arose from the fact that a lifelong diet of rich foods had encouraged an embolic condition. The corrective procedure was to take a segment of leg-artery and graft it to the base of the damaged heart artery, bypass the damaged tube and graft it to the upper, or outlet, end, where blood could then be pumped without undue pressure or without limiting the flow, into the heart.

Doctor Whalen finished speaking and threw up both hands in a little personal mannerism, meaning that was all there was to it. He then asked Charles Southcott who his personal physician was, and got a blunt answer.

'I don't have one. My wife goes to Philip Bourdon, but I haven't seen a physician in about ten years. Why?'

'To get the information about you,' said Whalen. 'To ascertain what your allergies are, if any. To know everything that may be pertinent, before surgery.'

Southcott had been weighing what Whalen had said earlier. He was, very cautiously, beginning to feel a breath of sweet hope. 'And after the surgery, after this re-routing of whatever you call it, has been done, Doctor, just how good will I be?'

Walter Whalen smiled. He had known that sooner or later some such question would arrive. 'Probably as good as any man your age, in your condition, is, who has not had the operation. There is probably some enlargement, naturally, since this condition has been chronic for a long while. You are responsible for that; you should have had a periodic, complete examination. But I would think you'll be able to see your grandchildren—at least as far as the heart is concerned.'

Doctor Whalen looked at his watch. He really was in no hurry but he did not like to repeat himself, and now that everything had been said, additional conversation was going to become repetitious. He stood up. 'The last time you saw a doctor, was it by any chance Philip Bourdon?'

Southcott nodded. 'Years ago.'

Walter Whalen departed. Like a detective, which was essentially what a general practitioner was, he went to an office telephone and called Doctor Bourdon, whom he knew only by reputation as a 'society physician', the kind that prescribed diet pills for overweight rich women, and who prescribed low cholesterol diets for over-indulgent rich men.

Bourdon remembered treating Charles Southcott. 'For a sprained Achilles tendon. But I don't have a file on him, and I doubt if anyone else has. He's one of those types that go

31

to physicians only when they can't breathe or stand erect ... there was one thing I remember about him. He told me of having knee surgery in college—I think it was a football injury, but of that I'm not sure. What I *do* remember though, because it seemed odd, was him telling me that he had nearly died from the anaesthesia; that he had some manner of near-fatal reaction that poisoned him.'

Doctor Whalen put the telephone upon its cradle very gently, an almost heretical thought trying to form in his mind. He returned to Southcott's room and asked about the knee surgery.

Southcott remembered. 'It wasn't the operation, that did not actually amount to much. I wasn't able to use the leg for the balance of that playing season, but within a month I was walking as well as ever. It was the damned anaesthetic; I had a very bad reaction to it. One of the doctors told me at that time that what I had amounted to more than allergy. It was more like catalytic reaction; something in my makeup which was probably entirely harmless by itself, turned to poison, or produced a poisoning effect, when any ether- or chloroform-type of anaesthetic was used on me.'

Doctor Whalen knew the symptoms, but he had never actually met anyone before in whom the reaction was this violent. 'There are other anaesthetics,' he said, 'that are not based upon either chloroform or ether. Quite a large number of them, in fact. We'll make tests, Mister Southcott.'

The financier accepted this. 'All right. But you be damned certain, Doctor. I barely made it through that other episode twenty years ago. And I was younger then.' Southcott's eyes suddenly brightened with an idea. 'Doctor; I wasn't just younger, I did not have a bad heart in those days. This time . . . I'm not going to tell you your business.'

Walter Whalen arose nodding. 'We'll take every precaution, Mister Southcott.'

'When will the operation be done, Doctor?'

Walter Whalen had no idea. Boston General had a number of surgical theatres, but it also had a large number of patients scheduled for surgery. 'I'll let you know later,' he said, and departed.

John Ames was finishing a conversation on a wall-telephone up the corridor and saw Walter Whalen emerge from the Southcott room. He waited, and when Doctor Whalen came along, he said, 'I have the reports on my desk. It doesn't look too bad for Southcott. Have you explained things to him?'

'Yes,' said Doctor Whalen, continuing to slowly pace the corridor.

'And you scheduled surgery?'

'No. I'm on my way to look into that now.' Whalen did not slacken his gait. 'He has an allergy to ether and chloroform derivatives.

33

Philip Bourdon told me about that; he treated him once for a sprained tendon.'

Doctor Ames thought nothing much of that. 'We'll just have to find an alternative,' he said. 'It's a wide open field.' Ames was more interested in Southcott's reaction to being told his condition could be corrected. 'Feeling sorry for himself, was he?'

'Maybe he was yesterday—don't they all? Today, except for this other thing, it looks like routine.' Whalen paced along, head down, face closed in private thought. As soon as he got clear of Ames he made the routine enquiry about a date and time for Southcott's surgery, then he went to the staff room and drew a cup of coffee, which he took to the rear-wall window, and there he sorted through the ideas that filled his mind.

John Ames would never stand for it, of course, and he would be supported by Boston General's staff. On the other hand there was a good argument for using the Whalen Innovation; Southcott's reaction to the derivatives of the traditional anaesthetics. But as Ames had said, there were alternatives; not all anaesthetics derived from ether and chloroform. But, if Southcott's system reacted adversely to the other things...

Walter Whalen sipped his coffee.

This could be the best opportunity he would have for years. What strengthened him in his feeling was the fact that Charles Southcott, knowing he could not tolerate the traditional anaesthetics, could probably be convinced they should employ Whalen's discovery. Of course Whalen would have to present this in such a way that Southcott would want to do it, and Whalen would have to accomplish this even if an alternate anaesthetic to which Southcott did *not* react adversely, were found—and that was dishonest. Walter Whalen would be capitalising on Southcott's ignorance. Maybe Southcott would not know this, but John Ames certainly would.

The temptation was very strong. Walter Whalen had no qualms because he knew positively that his innovation was qualified. And, he had to try it on a human being before it would achieve any kind of general acceptance.

He finished the coffee and went back for a second cup.

If Southcott insisted, John Ames could only forbid the Innovation's use on technical grounds, and Walter Whalen could rebut that objection with reams of catalogued proof of his experimental successes.

But it would be messy, and Ames would certainly seek Whalen's termination as an associate at Boston General.

But that would have to be the price Walter would be required to pay. No great innovator in history, as far as Walter could recall, ever avoided persecution and proscription of one kind or another. He smiled crookedly out the window. At least they could not break him on the rack nor burn him at the stake. He finished the coffee and went briskly back down the hall to Charles Southcott's room, organising his arguments and holding back the quick, hot flush of anticipation. There was one other element, but that was only a fringe benefit: if a man of Charles Southcott's stature were Doctor Whalen's first human success, he wouldn't really need any more. One enthusiastic Charles Southcott was worth a thousand itinerants who might be paid to allow themselves to be experimented upon. When Charles Southcott held a news conference every wire service in the world carried his story.

This, then, had to be exactly the opportunity Walter Whalen had needed, and, as he had thought earlier, if this one were allowed to slip away, it was not inconceivable that Whalen would never get another one as good.

He would have to face John Ames, of course, but even that was not a major deterrent, and if John got stubborn, which he most certainly would, then perhaps Charles Southcott could persuade him to step aside. Charles Southcott was the kind of man who would do that, too, even if he had to sign waivers, which everyone undergoing surgery at Boston General had to sign anyway, and even if Charles Southcott had to bring pressure on Ames, and that was another reason why Walter Whalen dared not allow this opportunity to slip away; Southcott was precisely the kind of man Walter Whalen needed. He was, in fact, the *only* kind.

But Mrs. Southcott was in the room when Doctor Whalen entered, and that scotched things, at least for the time being. Walter had to repeat what he had told Southcott earlier, for the benefit of his handsome wife. Then he had to give a plausible reason for returning, so he mentioned having arranged for the surgery as soon as possible, and departed, not as disappointed as he was impatient.

John Ames was gone when Doctor Whalen sought him in the administration offices, to take Ames to lunch. A secretary said Doctor Ames was in a conference with the directorship and probably would not be back downstairs for several hours, because those directors' meetings took forever, what with budgets and so forth being endlessly discussed.

Doctor Whalen was properly sympathetic, then he went out to lunch by himself, and for the first time in his life, felt dishonest, felt like a conspirator.

Conscience could be a terrible thing. So could the thought that everything he had dedicated his life to, up until now, was being put on the block, and that even if he succeeded, which was a foregone conclusion, it would cause a rift between Walter Whalen and John Ames—all the staff at Boston General—that would preclude his continuing there as an associate.

He did not want to have to pay that price, and yet if he were not willing to sacrifice *something*, what he knew for an absolute fact was the greatest discovery in the field of anaesthesiology since historic times, was very likely never going to be proved and adopted.

He consoled himself with the feeling that, given enough time, perhaps five or six years, John Ames and the others would come round. Then he told himself that whether they did or not, he *had* to do it, he had to persuade Charles Southcott to request the use of the Whalen Innovation.

By the time he finished lunch and was ready to return to Boston General, Margaret Morton Southcott would be gone, her husband would be alone, and with nothing more pressing on his agenda for the balance of the afternoon, Walter Whalen could take all the time he needed to convert Charles Southcott, and perhaps later, when John Ames returned and was told what Southcott's decision was, it would be too late for Ames to dissuade Southcott, if he tried. More probably John Ames would summon Walter Whalen to his office, and do the dissuading at that level.

And that, very definitely, was not going to succeed!

CHAPTER FIVE

THE FIRST AND SECOND HURDLES

The sequence of events went exactly as Doctor Whalen had thought they might. He used an hour, almost an hour and a half, convincing Charles Southcott that the Innovation was his best answer to allergic reaction to drugs, and he did it so completely that Southcott's enthusiasm overcame his natural skepticism. Southcott, the financier, was neither an entrenched conservative nor a flaming liberal, but he was enough of both, in delicate balance, to be successful where other men were afraid to run risks, and this was, in the end, what converted him, plus another factor that Walter Whalen suspected: Southcott liked Whalen, who was also a direct, energetic man.

At four o'clock when Doctor Whalen had the slip of paper on his desk giving the date and time for Southcott's scheduled surgery, he was summoned to the administrative office of the Chief Resident by a secretary whose voice sounded almost tremulous. He knew, as he put down the telephone, that John Ames knew; he could surmise without difficulty that John Ames had reacted in front of the girl who had telephoned Walter Whalen.

The weather was bad outside, the storm that

had struck one day previous, was not abating, but deep within Boston General the clinical serenity was untouched by that. Walter went to an office window and looked out, hands clasped behind him. His spirit was almost as troubled as the world beyond his window, and yet as he waited, giving Ames ample time to get calm and icy, which was how he always got eventually, after an outburst of temper, the hereditary indomitable Whalen temperament continued obdurate.

He knew about how the meeting was going to go, which saddened him a little, and he also knew that unless John Ames—or someone at any rate—dissuaded Charles Southcott, within a week or maybe a month, the Whalen Innovation was going to be called a revolutionary breakthrough in the field of medical anaesthesiology, and that was worth what he had to face now, as he left the office and slowly walked up front to the busy Administrative Section.

He knew, before he approached the door of the Chief Resident's office, he was being covertly stared at: this was his initiation, evidently. Rogue doctors were rare. When he opened the door John was behind his large, shiny desk with a cup of coffee on the pad in front of him. Their eyes met and Walter saw the iciness. Ames motioned towards a coffee urn on an antique little rosewood table. 'Help yourself, Walter.'

Whalen obeyed, feeling no desire for coffee at all. Then he faced the desk, cup in hand, and said, 'You may fire when ready, John.'

Ames did not explode. He had already done that. He pointed to a chair, which Walter declined to use, then he blew out a big sigh and said, 'How could you do it, Walter? You *know* you've known ever since that silly idea came up, there was absolutely no way it would be allowed.'

Whalen tasted the coffee. It was much better than the coffee in the staff room. 'John, believe me when I tell you it is absolutely safe, and in its own way, it is miraculous.'

Ames did not seem eager to argue. He was the kind of a man to whom friendships meant much. 'But Walter, not here. Not at Boston General, and not in any other community hospital I've ever heard of. I've told you time and again—we don't *have* any guinea-pigs. Now Walter, this must stop right here.'

'Even if Charles Southcott wants it?'

Ames turned slightly red in the face. 'I didn't believe it; I didn't believe you would do that. You deliberately sold him on this crazy idea of yours.'

'It's not crazy, John. I'll stake my life on it.' Walter finally crossed the room to the front of the desk. Ames had touched a nerve. 'It works every time, and it is absolutely fool-proof. John, I don't excuse my method, I'm only trying to—'

41

'I know what you're trying to do,' broke in Ames, arising behind the desk. 'But not here. I've told you that a dozen times.'

'And how do I prove it, then?'

Ames stuck to his point. 'Not here.'

Walter Whalen's temper rose a notch. 'John, Southcott wants it. He specifically volunteered. Listen a moment: if this man survives his surgery, and there's no reason why he shouldn't, he'll tell the press, he'll literally tell the world, that Boston General has a miraculous break-through in the field of anaesthesiology, and Boston General will be as prominent, then, as the Mayo Clinic up in Rochester.'

Ames turned towards a window, then turned back again. In a controlled, incisive tone he said, 'Walter, I'm not saying your—thing, whatever it is—won't work. I won't question your thoroughness in creating it, in perfecting it, but the basic issue is simply as I've said before a number of times, and which I'll say one more time: *Not here*! Do you understand? And I don't give a damn whether Mister Southcott volunteered—after you sold him—or not.'

Whalen drank coffee to gain time for his anger to atrophy. He even walked back to the little rosewood table and put the cup over there, before speaking again.

Then he turned and said, 'Southcott wants it. He believes, if you don't. John, I don't think you ought to oppose this man.'

Ames stiffened. 'That was a threat.'

Whalen returned to the area of the desk, his tone and look changing. 'Look; Southcott will sign waivers of responsibility. He's already agreed to absolve everyone—me, you, Boston General ... John, I have to have Charles Southcott. He can do everything for the Innovation it needs. He can—'

'He can,' exclaimed Ames, 'get the hell out of this hospital, is what Charles Southcott can do, if he persists ... and I don't want to say this, Walter, but if he *does* persist, you can get out right along with him.'

Whalen gripped the back of a chair until his knuckles whitened. 'I think,' he said, in a voice forced soft and steady, 'you had better not tell him that.'

Ames paused, but only for a long look at Whalen, then he spoke again. 'I *will* tell him that. And I'll also tell the directors, and the Staff ... my gawd, Walter, do you know what you're doing? Even without the publicity that may follow, if Southcott makes an issue of this, even without that, you're ruining your career. Don't do it, Walter. Medicine isn't like repairing automobiles; you can't just pick up your tools and walk down the street and get another job in another garage.'

'You're making a mountain out of a molehill,' said Whalen. 'There is absolutely *no danger*. John, come over to my place tonight and I'll prove everything I've claimed.'

Ames turned cold again. 'Everything I've said has gone right over your head, Walter. I don't *care* whether your invention works or doesn't work. That is *not* the issue, with me. You positively cannot use it here.'

Whalen did not retort. This was the sum and substance of their dispute and if they continued the discussion for another hour—or another week—they would only be recovering the same ground, something Walter Whalen did not like to do. He threw up his hands in that little characteristic mannerism of his, and stood quietly gazing at Doctor Ames.

'It rests with Charles Southcott, then,' he said, and turned toward the door.

Ames stopped him with an angry statement. 'Like hell it does. It lies with *me.*'

Walter reached for the knob. 'All right, John. But you're going to have to tell that to Mister Southcott.' He opened the door and passed on through, closed the door, and felt, again, the probing, covert stares.

When he reached the gleaming, white corridor that led down to a Nurses Station mid-way, and beyond, to a row of doors and a further corridor, nothing looked as it had looked a half hour ago. Everything, for the time being, that he saw or felt or heard, was different, was coloured by the inner discomfort he now felt, after the stormy session with his friend—his *ex*-friend.

It was quitting time anyway. He did not even go back and give his office a final glance, as was his custom. He left the building, caught his breath when the cold air struck, and ducked his head as he made his way to the parking area.

Well; he had done it. He regretted what had passed between John Ames and himself, but otherwise he had not a single regret, nor a single doubt. He did not even feel compelled to go home and try the innovation; it never failed and its procedure never deviated.

John Ames was a fathead. Exasperation made Walter Whalen think that. He liked John and he respected him immensely in his speciality, which was internal medicine. John was also probably the best hospital Chief Resident in all New England. At least he certainly was *one* of the best. But he was also the most pig-headed, stubborn, unreasonable man among Walter Whalen's lengthy list of acquaintances, associates, and friends.

Walter drove to a restaurant he frequented fairly often, and went first to the bar for a pick-me-up, which he definitely needed. The restaurant was exclusive and expensive, and therefore it was not crowded—it was *never* crowded.

The bartenders knew him, so did the waiters. So, in fact, did many of the patrons, but tonight he was not in a very affable mood, so, although he nodded and returned greetings, he sat hunched at the bar in the subdued lighting and sipped his drink, and had a second one which he also sat and sipped. It was the second one that brought a kind of mellowness, and with that mood taking him over, he went to the dining-room and had dinner.

Now—all that remained, was Charles Southcott. If John Ames could dissuade him, Walter Whalen was shot down in flames. John Ames could then move to have Walter disassociated from Boston General, and everything would then be in a fine shambles.

If Southcott could *not* be dissuaded, and Walter reflected long upon that possibility, believing he had rather thoroughly convinced Southcott, why then the battle was going to shift away from Walter and shift over to John Ames. In that kind of an engagement, Walter knew who would win: Southcott. Boston General's board of directors were, every one of them, prominent businessmen, investors, *entrepreneurs*. They were *not* medical men. For Walter Whalen this was a godsend.

But he winced from what would happen to John Ames. It had not been Walter's intention to have anything like that occur. Nor did it have to occur, if only John weren't such a fathead, weren't such a typical Englishman, with his mile wide bull-headed streak.

Walter thought fondly of Ames. When two men, particularly two unmarried men, had been friends as long as Whalen and Ames had been, there was more to it than just some similar likes and dislikes.

The consolation, or so Walter told himself, was that in time John would acknowledge his mistake. Maybe. John Ames was right, on his basic point: a hospital was not an experimental laboratory, and even after the Whalen Innovation was hailed throughout the international world of medicine, John was still going to be right: no matter how wonderful an innovation was, a community hospital was no place to try it first on people.

After dinner, Walter went back for a third highball at the bar, which was more of a load than he had carried in years. After that, he drove home through empty, storm-cowed streets feeling full and mellow and not a little melancholy.

Probably, a really wise man, left the discoveries to others, and remained comfortably in his niche. Particularly if his profession was as touchy upon the subject of ethics as was Whalen's profession.

That third highball had been a stout one. As Walter put up his car, despite the meal he had eaten, the reaction arrived and he had one hell of a time finding the keyhole in his front door, after leaving the garage and bucking an icy wind to the front of the house.

He leaned to get the door closed from the inside, flicked on lights, shed his hat and coat and stood a moment looking at his large and handsomely furnished living-room. What in the hell did a single man need with a place that exuded charm and good taste, wealth and culture—all of which had cost him a staggering sum to have the professional interior decorator organise like this—when he had no family and never entertained.

He swore at the beautiful room and went grumbling along to shower and get ready for bed. Once the damned innovation was being produced commercially, and he was raking in money with both hands, he damned well might just give up the practice of medicine anyway. Maybe go to Rome and become one of those rich, pampered expatriates.

If only Charles Southcott stuck to his guns.

CHAPTER SIX

RESOLVING THE CRISIS

Doctor Whalen was being called on the intercom. He heard it as he arrived quite late the next morning at Boston General. He had arrived late on purpose. He had thought it all through while lying abed much earlier, and had decided he would not arrive at the hospital until John Ames had had his opportunity to talk to Charles Southcott. Whalen had no stomach at all for intrigue and the kind of sub-rosa deceit he would probably have had to act out if he'd arrived earlier. Most of all, he had no stomach for debating his position before Charles Southcott, with Ames.

His attitude, as he went to the receptionist's desk and punched a button before lifting the telephone, was passive. He had done everything, the previous day, that had to be done. Now, it would lie with Southcott.

The call was a summons to Charles Southcott's room. Doctor Whalen put down the telephone without surprise and headed on through, first, to his office. There he left his hat and coat, put on his white jacket, skimmed through the notes atop the desk which had been left there by the night staff, and which touched upon relevancies among other patients he had an interest in, then he went along to Southcott's room in the private wing.

John Ames was not there, but he had been. Charles Southcott, looking fresh and alert—and curious—greeted Doctor Whalen with a brisk nod. Without any preliminaries he said, 'Well, Doctor, I'm afraid we've tossed a wrench in the works.'

Out of that sentence one word was reassuring: We. Whalen felt relief. 'I'm sure we have, Mister Southcott. You've seen Doctor Ames?'

Southcott gave a hard smile. 'I've seen him. And I've listened to him.'

'And?' said Walter Whalen, standing motionless but relaxed.

49

Southcott chose not to give a direct answer. 'Doctor; you have absolutely no misgivings about this invention of yours, none at all? You are absolutely positive there is no margin for error?'

Whalen's conviction came through strongly. 'Positively no margin for error, Mister Southcott. But that's not Doctor Ames's objection to it. And he's correct in theory: Boston General is not an experimental institution.'

Southcott looked a little baffled. 'All right. I understand this. But as I asked Doctor Ames— how the hell do people in his profession verify the desirability of something if they do not believe it should be tried the first time?'

Walter Whalen smiled. Southcott obviously had stuck to his guns. 'It's an interesting question,' he told Southcott. 'Of course it *has* to be tried, eventually. The common procedure is to buy a volunteer—something like that. Doctor Ames does not think you or any other patient in a community hospital, should be a guinea-pig.'

Southcott retorted with loud exasperation, and it was easy to imagine him saying this same thing to John Ames. 'Well, for Chris'sake, Doctor, the way I understand my situation here at Boston General, is that the corrective surgery is a standard thing, and that there's an excellent chance that it'll correct my ailment. But you know now, as well as I do, that with

50

my history of adverse reactions to anaesthetics, *that* could kill me where the surgery could not. So what in the hell is this argument all about?'

Walter Whalen had the answer in one word. 'Ethics, Mister Southcott.'

The burly man in the bed reacted to this as though it were some medieval curse. 'Doctor, do you know where the medical profession can shove their ethics, in this case?'

Whalen smiled and nodded his head. 'I can imagine. But Doctor Ames is our Chief Resident. His word is law.'

Southcott showed a different smile from his usual one. 'Is that a fact, Doctor? Well; his word may be law in *most* cases, but *not* where my life is concerned. Doctor Whalen, I want this surgery performed while I'm anaesthetised—or whatever the proper term is—by your method. Without any drugs. And I've already telephoned my wife to get hold of my legal firm to see that this is done. I've also talked to three members of your Board of Directors, and I've given them my solemn promise that if I'm anaesthetised by drugs, I'm going to sue this gawddamned hospital every Monday morning for the next ten years, until one or the other of us is bankrupt. I also told them that if they will have legal waivers drawn up, I'll sign them absolving the hospital and everyone connected with it from any responsibility whatsoever. Now what do you

51

say to *that*?'

Doctor Whalen made that little arm-flapping gesture of finality of his, and smiled. 'I would imagine we will proceed, using my innovation.'

Southcott bobbed his head. 'You better believe it. And so had Doctor Ames. And I'll tell you something else; I told Ames I want the operation moved up on his surgical schedule to tomorrow. No later than day after tomorrow. I want to get out of this medieval torture chamber as soon as possible.' Southcott studied Whalen's face for a moment, then gradually let his exasperation dwindle. In a calmer tone he said, 'Please don't think I'm throwing my weight around arbitrarily. I don't mean to bump someone else out of their place in line for an operation.'

Whalen could answer that easily. 'You won't be. Not really; Boston General has adequate facilities for its patients. It's not usually the number of patients that inhibit operations here anyway, it's the availability of surgeons.'

Charles Southcott's bedside telephone chimed and without taking his eyes off Whalen he reached and punched the 'hold' button. Then he said, 'I want you to answer just one question for me, Doctor: In all your experiments with this—discovery—of yours, have you ever had a single failure; by that I mean, has there ever been any malfunction of

52

the machine, or has there ever been a bad or contrary reaction on anything you've tried the thing on?'

'Never,' stated Whalen, with a ring of unshakable candour and confidence in his voice. 'I explained to you how it works, Mister Southcott; it is basically a very simple procedure. All it does, actually, is temporarily lift out your physical awareness. It disassociates you from your body by using electronic principles that simply have not been applied to the field of medical anaesthesiology before. It is really not all that fabulous: sooner or later someone else would have thought of it. The principles have been around for a long while; it has never failed, since I've been working with it, and I just don't see how it can fail.'

Southcott nodded briskly. 'I'm satisfied.' He reached for the telephone. 'Excuse me, Doctor.'

Walter Whalen left the room. Out in the corridor he probably should have felt the thrill of triumph, at least the sensation of satisfaction that he had won and that his innovation was going to get its chance. Instead, he felt depressed over Southcott's steamrollering of John Ames. He went back to his office, took the slips off the desk and began his rounds. He intended to wait until lunchtime before going to the Chief Resident's office. John probably would refuse his luncheon invitation, but at least he would make it, which would make him feel better.

Later, when he'd made the rounds, had exchanged his white jacket for his suit coat and had appeared in the administrative offices, he learned that Doctor Ames had left the hospital earlier, right after his bout with Mister Southcott in fact, and had not returned.

Obviously, John was going personally, before the directors to plead his case. Walter went to lunch alone, pitying Ames. Regardless of John's considerable and eminent standing in the medical field, he was not now dealing with men to whom this was going to be a determining factor. Doctors played by their rules, and businessmen played by theirs.

After lunch, Walter returned to Boston General, traded jackets again, and was about to leave his office when he had a telephone call from a man who identified himself as a member of Charles Southcott's legal firm. He wanted to discuss the technicalities of the innovation, and as Walter sat back explaining, he could tell from this attorney's questions and comments that he was just as much at home in the field of electronics as he was in the field of law.

At the conclusion of this twenty-minute conversation the lawyer did not come right out and commit himself in favour, which Walter hardly expected, lawyers being lawyers, but the man *did* say he wished he had thought of the thing, and Walter smiled to himself about that: no one not closely connected with medicine, particularly with anaesthesiology and its unpleasant side-effects, would have any reason to think of it.

He was completing some paper work at one of the Nurses' Stations shortly before three o'clock in the afternoon when the summons came from Administration. He could not anticipate, this time, so his heart missed a beat as he started up the long corridor. John Ames had returned, that much was evident since the summons had come from his office. Otherwise though, Doctor Whalen entered the outer office without any fore-knowledge, but with a definite sense of foreboding.

John was talking on the telephone when Walter entered. He did not, as was customary, wave Walter to a chair. He looked over the telephone at Whalen from a totally expressionless face, then completed his conversation and replaced the telephone upon its stand as he said, 'Southcott's surgery will be at seven o'clock tomorrow morning.'

Walter stood braced for what came next. Ames let him wait while he crossed to the urn and drew himself a cup of coffee. He did not invite Whalen to have a cup, he simply paced back behind his desk and raised his head, looking as distant and uncompromising as ever.

'And your innovation will be used.'

Walter let his body go loose from head to feet. He had won. In a quiet, everyday tone of voice he said, 'I missed you at lunch, John.'

It did not work. Ames was not to be placated; he was not accepting any olive branches today from Walter Whalen. 'Southcott's lawyers are sending over non-responsibility waivers. Our attornies are working on the same angles.' Ames drank some coffee and put the cup atop his desk. 'Walter, everyone is going to be in the clear but you. The directors have protected themselves. I've gone on record as being absolutely opposed to this thing, and I've disassociated myself from it, from you, and also from Boston General, for the length of time Southcott will be in surgery. It's your little ball game. Yours and Southcott's. I wish you both well.'

'Thanks,' said Whalen. 'Mind if I have some coffee?'

In the same crisp tone of detachment he had been using, Ames said, 'Help yourself ... any point in a last minute appeal, Walter?'

Whalen pulled a crooked smile. 'As though I'm going to the wall, John?'

'That is exactly what you are doing, Walter, in the professional sense. Win or lose, you've broken faith with our vocation. Can you imagine re-locating somewhere under those circumstances? And I don't give a damn whether your innovations sweeps the medical

56

world and brings you all manner of fame—and probably fortune as well, if you can interest a manufacturer in making and selling the things—you are still gong to appear among other professional people as a man whose lack of self-discipline, and ethics, has made him an undesirable.'

Walter got the coffee and turned in exasperation. 'For Chris'sake, John, these are the seventies, not the twenties. People aren't still going round with stiff upper lips and exaggerated concepts of honour and whatnot. Nowadays, people want to get on with it; they want to be involved with the facts of living, not with a lot of silly anachronistic crap. You're talking like someone from another time. If you want my resignation from staff, you can have it after tomorrow, but my guess is that after tomorrow the directors, and the younger members of staff would be more favourable to having *your* resignation. Nothing succeeds like success, ethics and all that other rubbish notwithstanding.'

John Ames did not change in any noticeable way. He finished his coffee, waited until Walter Whalen had finished his, then he went over and held the office door open without speaking and without nodding, as Doctor Whalen walked out.

That was the break between two old friends. Walter returned for his suit-coat to the office, then he left Boston General for home. He did not even notice that the week-long storm had gone, that although it was cold and brisk and very still outside, and the day was drawing to an early close, the sky was as clear as smoked glass and much more transparent.

He did not even drive home with conscious effort, nor did he remember doing it, as he went to the kitchen to prepare supper for himself. All he thought about was the loss of a friend, which was painful, and what he had to do next morning. For one thing, with Southcott's surgery scheduled that early—seven o'clock— Walter would have to get up at five; not a very pleasant prospect at any time, but particularly not a pleasant prospect in early winter.

CHAPTER SEVEN

'WALTER—CONGRATULATIONS'

Nothing was really very different the following morning when Doctor Whalen arrived at Boston General, unless it was the businesslike silences he encountered, the crisp efficiency, but then that was not altogether unusual at any time and especially it was not unusual when there was a surgery slated in which he would be involved.

Chief Surgeon was Leon Swansinger, a very good man. Swansinger's back-up-man was to be Spencer Littleton, also a good man. Otherwise, there would be the usual crew, except that while the customary anaesthesiologist would be present, Doctor Walter Whalen would take over at that position.

John Ames was not present during the short and brisk pre-surgical briefing, but then he rarely ever was, so Doctor Whalen did not miss him. As he went into the operating room he wondered if John had actually avoided coming in this morning as he had said he would do. It seemed a little absurd to go to such a length just to prove that he did not want to have anything to do with what was going to happen. But then, completely hostile people were never entirely *not* absurd.

Swansinger and Littleton were friendly but noticeably reticent. Even when Walter took the Innovation from its small leather case and placed it upon a stainless-steel table, and ran out the extension cord to a wall-socket and plugged it in, they watched with something like bland interest, and did not ask a single question. Walter was annoyed; Leon Swansinger was in charge from this moment on. When the patient was wheeled in, Swansinger was responsible for everything that ensued. He should, Walter thought, have asked for a complete explanation of the principle and the function of the small metal instrument atop the stainless-steel table, since

59

Swansinger was going to be wrist-deep in Charles Southcott's chest very shortly now.

Swansinger, though, joined Spencer Littleton in an inventory of everything else, first, and only came round to Doctor Whalen's position last. Then, finally, and with an ironic variety of calm blandness that would have been insulting and infuriating another time, he laid a hand atop Whalen's small metal box and leaned to look at the rheostat knob and the needle-gauge used only to verify that enough, and not too much, electrical current was being transmitted from the wall-outlet to the Innovation. In a tone of voice he might have used to a child, Swansinger said, 'Well, Walter, what have we here?'

Whalen nearly took his head off. 'Are you being smart, Leon?'

Swansinger's face underwent a complete change. He removed his hand from the metal box and said, 'Walter, you had better be absolutely right about this thing, and I mean it, because we're not removing tonsils this morning. Once you signal me Southcott is under, I'm going into his chest. If anything goes wrong, if he suddenly comes out of it and moves or does anything that could make my hand slip, he's going to be the deadest bastard you ever saw—and *you* are going to be the murderer.'

Swansinger stepped away and returned to the side of his back-up surgeon, young Spencer

Littleton. Swansinger had delivered his non-responsibility waiver personally and orally, and he had also shown Walter just exactly how he felt behind that mask of blandness.

Littleton would undoubtedly share his chief's sentiments. Walter glanced at the other members of the surgical team, and those who met his glance did so stonily. He began to feel quite alone even in the midst of a small crowd. Then they brought Charles Southcott in. Normally, he would have been sedated to a degree of lethargic, or euphoric, drowsiness. Now, he raised his head and with a commanding sweep of the room, settled his stare upon Doctor Whalen. He winked. Walter was not alone after all. He waited until Southcott had been transferred to the operating table, then picked up the spring-steel, adjustable band and stepped up to make it fit snugly but not tightly around Southcott's head an inch above the temple, exactly as he had fitted the band dozens of other times, except that initially, when he'd experimented on rodents, he'd used a one-shot taping system, which had been satisfactory on small creatures, but which he had happily discarded when he'd graduated to larger animals, in favour of the adjustable spring-steel band with its four individual adjustable wing-nuts.

Charles Southcott did not move while the band was being adjusted in place. Afterwards, he raised a hand to feel the thing, And he grinned at Walter. 'On a clear day I ought to be able to receive Manila.'

Whalen smiled, but across the table Doctor Swansinger stood erect and uncompromisingly bleak. 'Mister Southcott,' he said, 'if I were you I would not go through with this.'

Southcott, conditioned to instantaneous antagonism by now, snapped his answer. 'All right, Doctor, then wait until you *are* me, then don't do it.'

'This operation, Mister Southcott, is normally a routine procedure based upon considerable successful precedents—using proved techniques.'

'Then get on with it,' growled Southcott, fixing Leon Swansinger with his hostile gaze. 'And have a little faith in your associate, Doctor Whalen. Now let's not have any more of this.'

Swansinger continued to look downward. Spencer Littleton moved in without a sound and so did the surgical nurse. The normal machinery began to hum, to warm up. Open-heart surgery of this type was, as Swansinger had said, fairly routine, but it was also a very delicate and complicated procedure requiring complete co-ordination between the team and their mechanical adjuncts.

For the officiating surgeons there was a respite while everything else was got ready. Neither of them spoke, and neither of them looked over at Doctor Whalen, who was

62

standing uncomfortably aside, ready to turn up the rheostat and lift Charles Southcott's consciousness out of his body.

Walter's palms were wringing wet. He had every confidence, every reason to believe—to know for a fact—that his Innovation was going to perform as it always had before. But there was one element that was new; he had never tired the Innovator on a human being before.

Swansinger looked up and said, 'Doctor Whalen...?'

Walter saw Southcott move his head the slightest bit. Rather than meet the man's eyes, Walter turned his back and leaned to be certain exactly the proper amount of electrical current was coming, then he firmly gripped the knob and began turning it. Southcott did not move for a moment or two, did not show an awareness of anything unusual or different, but as the rheostat kept turning Charles Southcott's body gradually began to stiffen and his eyes, fixed to the overhead lights with an almost deathly rigidity, widened a little at a time.

The sensation was neither pleasant nor unpleasant, it was simply totally different from anything Southcott had ever experienced or had ever imagined. It was a little like being weightless, like letting the body lie loose and relaxed in a vast pool of water, but with two particular differences; there was also a sensation of suction, or something like that, a feeling as though within his consciousness somewhere and somehow, a layer of him was being very gradually peeled away. That was one of the sensations. The other one was of a gradually descending weightiness that replaced the earlier weightlessness, as though the full force of atmospheric pressure was being applied per square inch over every part—not of his body, but of his mind, of his awareness. It was a kind of dull, thick, solid weightiness.

But none of this was really unpleasant. At first it worried him, even frightened him, but as the sensations increased he lost his fear; became immersed in a thick, heavy, dull kind of intellectual apathy. It was not unpleasant at all, once this sensation settled into place.

But there was no feeling of pleasantness either. The sum effect was of sinking under a tremendous weight which would make his legs and arms brutishly slow and ponderous in movement, which would turn his mind into channels more commensurate with some variety of primaeval being.

He heard Doctor Whalen say, 'Test his reflexes, please,' as though Whalen were a thousand miles, or years, away, and as though his distinguishable words were a whimper or a growl, but not things arranged as a result of human sequential thought with definite meaning.

The answer came shortly. 'He is under.'

Whalen stepped in and looked down, made a test himself by prying the eyelid up and looking intently, then said, 'Doctor Swansinger . . . ?'

Both the surgeons came up. Charles Southcott was there, eyes still rigidly fixed overhead, pulse and respiration perfectly acceptable, conscious in every way except that, obviously, he was not there at all, and Swansinger gave his head a light wag as though to say he had not believed it would work. Then they went to work, all of them, in perfect co-operation.

Charles Southcott could feel only the superficial things, the clamps, the fluttering fingertips, the passing light and shadows. Otherwise there was something inside his head that completely captured all his remaining, very small and under-developed, attention. It was sound, but not sound he heard, sound that he *felt* in a most peculiar way. Sound that searched out and filled every limit and pocket and niche of his awareness, excluding everything else, but especially excluding pain.

Once, Swansinger looked at the little box on the table and raised his eyes to Walter Whalen, but he said nothing.

The operation which had started out as a routine bit of sophisticated surgery, except for Whalen's innovation, settled into the procedural routine as though nothing being done in the operating room were different in

65

any way.

Spencer Littleton, a few years younger than Swansinger, and of a different temperament as well, smiled once at Walter. That was the only scrap of encouragement there was throughout the entire agonising ordeal.

As far as Walter Whalen was concerned, he was not a surgeon and though he'd seen much surgery, he did not enjoy being a participant. It was one of those things physicians had to be associated with, one of those interludes physicians were called upon to be associated with, and therefore they did it, but Walter Whalen had never enjoyed surgery the way some practitioners did. And today he liked it even less. Under the green gown his chest was covered with perspiration. His face too; he was damper than Leon Swansinger, who should have felt the nervous tension more than anyone present.

Some of Doctor Whalen's queasiness was attributable to the surgery itself, but most of it was the result of inescapable anxiety over what he was doing there, what he was proving there, and even though it was by now very obvious that he had been correct in every way, had been thoroughly justified in having the confidence he had never failed to feel, nevertheless this was his initial trial using a human being. Not just any human being, but using one of the nation's most prominent and outstanding financiers.

By ten o'clock when Littleton was sent in to

make the closure, Walter Whalen felt as though he had been on his feet for forty-eight hours. He was as wrung out with exhaustion as he had ever been in his life. There was still a little while yet to go.

Swansinger came round and stood looking from the little metal box to Walter. As much of Swansinger's face as was visible above the mask, showed a depth of his customary calm, but lightly influenced now with a kind of wary, or neutral, interest.

'Your procedure for ending the unconsciousness, Walter, he said quietly, 'is, as I understand it, bringing the decibel level back to normal, very gradually. Is that correct?'

Whalen nodded. Evidently John Ames had briefed Swansinger. 'That's correct, Doctor.'

Swansinger shifted his attention again to the little box. 'It looks so damned simple, Walter.'

'It is. It's very simple. Instead of stunning the mind or stupefying the consciousness with poison, which is what traditional anaesthetics do, Doctor, it simply separates the awareness from the body through an application of electronics. A high school boy could make one of these things.'

Leon Swansinger smiled for the first time. 'Yes. About the same way a high school boy could make an egg stand on end in Spain four or five hundred years ago—after a teacher named Christopher Columbus showed him

67

how to crack the lower end. Walter—congratulations.'

Whalen glowed.

'What is your next procedure?' Swansinger asked, looking casually round where Spencer Littleton was working over Charles Southcott.

'I'll carry the innovation right along with me and accompany the patient to Intensive Care,' said Whalen. 'I'll stay with Mister Southcott until this evening, or until such time as I believe it will be safe to turn the rheostat down and return him very gradually to consciousness.'

Doctor Swansinger nodded and looked into Whalen's face with a little expression of soft irony. 'Ames is going to feel foolish and look foolish, I'm sorry to say.' Doctor Swansinger turned and headed towards the door marked 'Exit'.

CHAPTER EIGHT

APPARENT SUCCESS

The surgery was a complete success. As Spencer Littleton trudged along beside Walter Whalen, he gave Walter a run-down. There had been enlargement, but not significantly; at least not dangerously, and otherwise the grafting had been entirely satisfactory. To Spender Littleton, as to Leon Swansinger, in this instance success was routine, and so were the discoveries made when Charles Southcott had been opened up.

Littleton went right along to the room previously put in readiness for Mister Southcott. He was interested in Walter's invention, and although he could not have heard Swansinger's parting statement to Walter in surgery, he said almost the identical thing before finally departing.

'Ames is going to look pretty darned stuffy over this.'

Doctor Whalen could not avoid feeling some sense of pride and triumph; he even felt a little condescending pity for John, but he had never been a vindictive person. As soon as he could, he'd go to see John. After all, so far at least, none of this had got out. Southcott's legal people and his wife knew about it, otherwise the lawyers who protected Boston General against malpractice suits and so-forth, were the only outsiders who had any inkling Charles Southcott's surgery had been accomplished by means of a completely radical and hitherto untried anaesthesiological procedure.

John could eat a little crow around the hospital, which he might even deserve, but otherwise no one would know of his mistaken and stubborn opposition.

Southcott was breathing in deep sweeps, as normally as anyone ever breathed. His pulse was good, his appearance was fair, and his colouring was superior to the colouring of anyone Doctor Whalen had ever seen after surgery, who lay drugged and inert from chemical anaesthetics.

There was a statuesque middle-aged dark-eyed nurse in private attendance, and from time to time people arrived to silently look in, then silently withdraw.

Walter sat, thick legs pushed out, body running all together, or at least feeling as though it were, upon a little metal chair facing the side of the bed. The metal box was atop a bedstand and the lighted 'On' switch glowed with little more brightness than a firefly made on a dark June night.

The statuesque private nurse took pity and brought Walter a cup of coffee. He was grateful. He would have been even more grateful if the coffee had been fortified with something, but she did not make that suggestion and Walter did not ask about it.

Doctor Swansinger arrived two hours later and seemed a little surprised to discover that Walter had not yet turned down the rheostat. Walter's explanation was valid. 'When he comes out from under it will be suddenly. With the usual anaesthetics he would return gradually, and be groggy for an additional two or three hours or more. This way, when he comes out of it, Leon, he will be looking and feeling exactly as he was when they wheeled

70

him into surgery, and therefore I like the idea of allowing his body as much time as it needs to adjust to all the cutting and sewing. I don't want him to move suddenly when he comes back.'

Doctor Swansinger, dressed in sport attire and ready, or so it appeared, for an afternoon of golf, leaned and studied the patient. 'Good colour, Walter,' he remarked. 'I suppose in time we'll get used to seeing them lying like this with their eyes wide open, won't we? Good pulse.' Swansinger turned, smiling. 'We must have done a good job on Mister Moneybags . . . Walter; I was thinking, while I was cleaning up. In order to market this thing of yours a good bit of capital outlay will be required.' Swansinger smiled and went as far as the door before finishing his statement. 'Unless you plan to work out some kind of royalty-deal with some manufacturer of surgical equipment, and in case you are thinking in terms of forming a company, I'd like to buy in. Bear that in mind, will you?'

Walter nodded. 'I'll bear it in mind. Are you by any chance leaving the building?'

'I am, yes. Why; is there something I can get you?'

'No. But if you happened to see John up in Administration, would you tell him I'd like very much to see him.'

Swansinger nodded and left, but a half hour passed without John Ames arriving, so

71

evidently he had chosen not to heed Whalen's appeal, or else he had not yet returned to the hospital.

This was the only haunting after-effect, everything else had turned out better than everyone excepting Whalen, had expected.

Finally, along towards evening when his strength had returned, he called in the private nurse to say he was going to bring Mister Southcott round and would require her in attendance, then, and thereafter. He did not want Mister Southcott to move. Not so much as one arm or one leg. She was to stand at bedside and tell that to Mister Southcott; she was to be certain of his attention, then to repeat that over and over to him until she was quite satisfied he understood, then she was not to leave him until she was satisfied he would remain immobile.

The nurse was a disciplined woman. Whatever she had heard *via* the inevitable grapevine she kept from showing in her expression or her manner, and now, although she seemed, or at least Doctor Whalen *thought* she seemed, slightly uneasy she moved to bedside and lightly lay a hand upon Southcott's right forearm.

Walter began very gently turning down the rheostat. By this time Charles Southcott had been in a state of some kind of detached suspension for twelve hours, since seven that morning until six the same day, in the evening.

In every way that was relevant, he was doing very well. Walter continued to gently bring down the decibel level and finally, when there could be no sound emanating, he removed the band from Southcott's head, placed it beside his metal box, and with a soft sight, flicked off the switch.

It had been silent in the room before, but not as silent, as eerily and empty silent, as it now seemed to be. Walter pulled the plug and began reeling in the great length of electrical cord, winding it round and round his metal box. The nurse spoke in almost a whisper from bedside.

'Doctor, his eyes are watering, his face is relaxing.'

Whalen knew the signs. 'He can hear you, so start your instructions.' Walter finished with the electrical cord and as the nurse began repeating her admonition to Charles Southcott, Walter sauntered over and looked closely at the patient.

Southcott looked perfectly normal in every way, except that he lay motionless and expressionless. He reacted through instinct to an excessive watering of the eyes by blinking rapidly and often, indicating he was in complete command, but unwilling quite yet to speak or turn his head, and Walter was satisfied that these things were the result of the instructions the nurse was still repeating to him.

As far as Walter was concerned, he had done

it. He had proved his procedure upon a human being, and had ended exactly as he had never for one moment doubted but that was how it would end.

He was hungry and tired, and he needed a drink, so he put the metal box in its leather case, told the nurse to call the Night Duty Resident if she needed anything, and in the event of an emergency to call him at home, or to have the Night Duty Resident call him, and left.

The corridors of Boston General were ordinarily lighted by day as well as by night, so when he struck out down the corridor to his office to change before leaving, he had no impression of the lateness. But twenty minutes later, when he emerged into the crisp, cold darkness, it struck him, and that made him feel even more tired.

The drive home was a mixture of actions and reactions. Finally, he felt grimly, almost defiantly, pleased with himself. While he had to concentrate on traffic, of which there was quite a bit at this time of evening almost any night, in Boston, he could also drift in a detached manner back and forth between what he had accomplished, and what this could mean in terms of his future.

Success was able to trigger a release of adrenalin, to make a man feel invincible and magnanimous. It was more of a 'lift' than liquor, or most drugs which were supposed to

74

do the same thing. Liquor was actually a depressant, and as far as the drugs were concerned, even the 'uppers', the ones designed to exalt the ego, had a let-down after-effect, but Walter Whalen's feeling on the drive home was purer and more enduring. Success convinced him more than ever that he had created something the world, the race of mankind, had needed for centuries. And this sensation never left him after he drove away from Boston General, although it got a jolt when, after he'd been home a couple of hours, Doctor Hammond who had the night-duty, called him to report that Charles Southcott had come round, and had elected not to obey instructions very well.

'It may,' said Doctor Hammond, 'be simply that, having no ill after-effects, no pain to speak of, that he believes himself better off than he is, but he has been troublesome. He wants to go home, and that'll be out of the question for some time yet.'

Walter said, 'Sedate him, Doctor.'

Hammond was agreeable. 'Of course. But that's really why I called. Is it possible that he's allergic to any particular sedative drug? I could find nothing to that effect on his record, but that probably only means no tests were run.'

As a matter of fact no such tests had been made, but Walter was not very troubled. He explained that only the older, more traditional anaesthetic derivatives had poisoned

75

Southcott in the past, advised mild sedation, which was all that would be required to bring on placidity, and named several synthetics that he felt sure would do the job.

Doctor Hammond was equally as confident, but, as he said, Charles Southcott was Walter's patient from here on; he had simply wanted to be sure Walter would approve and agree. Then, when Walter asked how Southcott was, otherwise, Doctor Hammond said, 'I've never seen anyone that looks so well after major surgery, Doctor Whalen. I think it's almost miraculous, what you've accomplished. The entire night crew is talking about it.' Hammond chuckled. 'It's being said Boston General is going to become as famous for the brilliance of its staff as Mayo's in Minnesota. One of the interns is going round claiming that your name should be submitted to the nomination committee of the Nobel organisation for the annual award in medicine.'

Walter laughed. 'It's not that great a thing, Doctor Hammond. In fact, it's nothing but an application of a very old electronic principle.'

'Whatever it is,' said Hammond, 'I want to extend my congratulations, too. As for Southcott, I'll see that he's sedated.'

'Call back if there are complications,' said Walter, and rang off. There would be no complications, he was quite certain, as long as no one overlooked the memo on Southcott's record, and no one would; the people at Boston General were never haphazard.

He went to the kitchen, put some coffee on to boil, put a frozen dinner in the oven to thaw, then went on through to the bar and mixed himself a mild one and took it with him to the back bedroom where he stripped to shower. He also took the highball into the shower with him, which was where he finished it.

Later, returning to the kitchen in pyjamas and gown, he ate his dinner, cleaned up the mess, then went on through to watch the news on television, and for once the imminence of war between India and Pakistan, the Arab-Israeli struggle, the depressing trivialities such as America's adverse balance of payments, Britain's threat to pull out of the Common Market, and East Germany's acquisition of a nuclear strike force, did not depress him at all. He sat there and listened to the gloom for half an hour, and arose, eventually, to retire, feeling better than he had felt in a very long while.

He lay awake calmly going over in his mind the opportunities that were now available to him, and during the course of all this very pleasant speculation he neglected even once, to think of John Ames.

Finally, he slept, and because of the exhaustion resulting from this very long and arduous day, he slept like a log.

This day, then, was the culmination of three years of experimentation and success, and a little more than one year of frustration and exasperation. He slept with a completely serene subconsciousness. He did not dream; there was no smouldering doubt, no anxiety at all, to prompt dreams.

There was no medicine on earth as completely efficacious as the sensation of success, for either the ill or the well.

CHAPTER NINE

THE FANTASY THAT WASN'T

The Rio Ebro began somewhere far to the northeast in the stony Calabrian Mountains, and on its course downward towards the Golfo de Valencia—the Gulf of Valencia—it gathered strength where the rivers Arga and Aragon junctured with it, and again, much nearer the gulf, it accumulated additional water from the rivers Cinca and Segre. After that, it flowed directly into the Mediterranean on a southeasterly course, making possible a green-belt on each side of its breadth that, had the land of peninsular Catalonia been less stony, would certainly have contributed to a flourishing agricultural economy. But the land was very old, and in most places very tired from continual cropping without putting back any of the nutrients which had been removed

78

over the millenias, along with being stony and mountainous, and mainly shallow.

But this was how God had made it. He had also made the mountains as well, and while they grudgingly yielded to the ingenuity of man, they never did this in any kind of abundance, hence the people who remained, who did not go to the industrial places like Barcelona and Gerona, or down to Valencia, lived very little different from the way their grandfathers and great-grandfathers had lived.

People understood how this had to be so. Chemical fertilisers helped, of course, and so did mechanisation, except that here too, the hand of God was clearly visible; if the ground did not yield much, then there was no money with which to buy the miracles of the Twentieth Century, the chemical fertiliser nor the mechanical devices, so, it all came back to the fact that the land was poor, and going back further, this was the Will of God, and that ended it.

A man could lie all day upon the slopes that stood bulwark-like facing the Mediterranean, and see the richer land which was green and cultivated, that ran unevenly along the coastline, but that was all a man could do who herded sheep and goats, and tended a few citrus and olive trees for a living, because that was very expensive land, down there. It was also too settled, too alive with people and activity, with demands made upon a man.

Well; God ordained where a man was born and how he was to live, and as Father Ordoñez had once said, within the hearing of Juan Valdez, but not to him, to someone else, the surest way to hell was to rebel against one's fate.

The village lay below, slightly to the southeast over nearer the river, which was probably why it had been founded where it still stood; life without water was not possible.

A man could see the rooftops, the dusty, ancient roadways, the people and the animals, the orange and olive trees, the latter dusty-coloured and spidery with a familiar grace, and he could hear soft sounds rising upwards along the fluted slopes. Villa Real, so it was said, had been created before the Romans; it had lived through Catalonia's turbulent history, and at one time it had been the place where a great lord had been put to death, his crime having been an endeavour to create from his dukedom an independent nation. Catalonia, he had said—and it was still mentioned now and again—was not Spanish, it was Catalonian, and if the Spanish could become a nation, then why not the Catalonians as well?

That was history. Villa Real was steeped in it, but all history did for a man who watched his flock upon the rough slopes, was made him conscious of the shortness of one lifetime. Even had Juan Valdez been a forceful person, a man unable to be influenced and dictated to, he would still have been imbued with the fatalism, not only of his race and his heritage, but also of his personality, for Juan Valdez was a passive man, gentle and friendly and of a soft heart lacking formidableness.

God was also responsible for this. Most young men went down to the factories or the mines, or to the fishing fleets, and whether they returned with good clothing and money or never returned at all—which most did not— had no effect whatsoever upon Juan Valdez, whose philosophy was easy and without stress. What God willed, a man did, and in the end he was better off.

The goats were above Juan Valdez; they were more nimble than the sheep, nor did they complain as much although they were just as garrulous. This place was familiar to them; it provided a variety of sustenance, not as good as other places but adequate, except that, of course, when they chewed things, because the ground was stony, they also chewed rock-dust, and eventually this wore their teeth down so that they could no longer be thrifty, then they were sold for money or were butchered for food.

Well; if this was the will of God, as were all things, why then a man accommodated himself to it, too. Juan Valdez, the only reasoning creature within some distance of where he lay, was content. He was a poor man, a shepherd who lived in the stone house left

81

him by his father, but poverty was something a man wore, it did not necessarily have to be any deeper than his old trousers or his threadbare shirt and jacket, while on the other hand contentment was a delicious feeling that abided deep within a man. He was content, and so he slept. It was afternoon, Maria knew where to find him, if she came, as she usually did, the flock was perfectly safe, the day was golden with a faint salt breeze, a man's life upon earth was not long, and all things considered, there was much in favour of a man being passive and content and malleable.

Juan Valdez drowsed off to sleep thinking of Maria Peralta, and when Charles Southcott awakened, or returned, or at least had the peculiar sensation of settling-in again, or settling-back again, he was also thinking of Maria Peralta, but in a different way, not passively nor lazily, certainly not with any malleability of thought because Charles Southcott had never been a malleable person; on the contrary, he had always been forceful, assertive, dominant. He was not altogether that way now, when he awoke upon the slope overlooking the village of Villa Real; something had blended, somehow, to ameliorate his lifelong and characteristic forcefulness. He was the same, and yet different. He was as strong and decisive as ever, but gentler, more susceptible to the needs and ideas of others. He was also too stunned when he opened Juan Valdez's eyes to dwell upon inner changes, because the external ones overwhelmed him. Actually, they frightened the hell out of him.

The goats, the breathtaking view, the odour of animals, the rooftops, the church spire, the dust and antiquity. *Villa Real!* He remembered the village vividly, only he had never before recalled its name. Three years ago on a side-trip from France. He was dreaming, of course. The hand he raised, the itch he felt under the ribs, the sensation of hot sunlight filtering downward through tree-branches, were parts of a most incredibly realistic dream.

He lay as still as death scarcely breathing, struggling to locate and hold down an elusiveness that evaded all his best efforts. He wanted to awaken, to be in Boston General again. *That* was real; *this* was *not* real. He concentrated on wakening but nothing happened. He finally sat up, willing himself to move, to be active in some restless way because that seemed the most probable way to leave a dream. But he was *there* and nothing he did or thought, or willed with all the power of his capability, changed anything.

A horned goat came to stand with its forefeet upon a large rock, ruminating furiously while it gazed directly at him with odd eyes, their colour was amber and there was a black line directly across them. The goat had brown-stained hair, like a narrow beard, suspended below its narrow jaw. It made a chuckering soft sound as though it knew him. And it continued to stand in that uninhibited posture, chewing and staring.

There were other goats and sheep, several of the latter black and stubby-legged and ungainly-looking, around the slope above and below him.

He studied himself in uncertain detachment. His trousers were too large. They were baggy and a kind of neutral tan colour. His shirt was almost worn through and none too clean, as was the jacket he wore. His skin was dark, his body lean with a litheness burly Charles Southcott had never known, but he had known men built like that and had admired their suppleness.

The thing that distracted him from this personal appraisal was the grating of loose shale under shoe-leather. An old man was descending the slope to his right a dozen yards. The old man had grizzled, grey beard-stubble and sweat on his mahogany face. He was carrying a patched remnant of what could have been sail-canvas slung over one shoulder. Whatever he had been gathering farther up the mountainside was inside the canvas.

The old man smiled and lifted his free hand in a little salute. 'You sleep like a stone, Juan Valdez,' he sang out, obviously much amused. 'The bell rang an hour back.'

Charles Southcott understood perfectly; it

did not—right then—occur to him that what he understood without trouble was a language which he did not know a single word of: Catalonian Spanish. He returned the old man's wave and called over saying, 'Did it?'

He watched the old man all the way down the slope to the uppermost environs of the tiled-roofed, and stone-slab village, marvelling at the total fidelity of this dream. It was frighteningly real. There was none of the broken sequences, the incomprehensible switches in continuity, of most dreams he'd had, and it had a depth of solid and unshakable reality, which was what still held him numb even an hour after he had awakened.

As a matter of fact Charles Southcott rarely dreamed. As a child he had, but not afterwards, in his later years.

In *this* delusion he could understand everything, could smell the dust and feel the sunheat, and he could actually hear the rumbling of his empty stomach.

Juan Valdez? But that was no stranger, then the fact that he knew that old man, whose name was Emilio Sanchez; he knew also that old Sanchez had been in the War, had been a *Falangist*, was a widower with a daughter who had left the village fifteen years earlier and had never been heard of since. He was sorry for Emilio Sanchez; everyone was sorry for the old man, even though everyone, as well as Juan

Valdez, understood exactly that it was God's will, all that had come to beset the old man.

The horned goat gave up and went down to join the other animals. He had been interested in Juan Valdez, obviously because he knew it was the time when the shepherd customarily drove his band back to the corral on the outskirts of the village. Goats, sheep, all animals, were strong creatures of established habit. Charles Southcott understood, finally, what the goat had been trying to convey to him: it was time to leave the mountainside.

He also knew where he was to go, where he would drive his flock.

This was the most insane gawddamned dream anyone ever had. He drew up Juan Valdez's sinewy legs and hooked both arms around them staring down at the rooftops. *Whalen! Doctor Whalen!* That is what this was all about. Doctor Whalen's crazy innovation, that was supposed to be so foolproof. What in the hell had Whalen *done* to him?

He should have suspected; now that he thought back, Whalen had repeatedly said that he had never had a failure, with experimental *animals*. Good God Almighty!

He did not hear the call the first two times, but the third time it came, as sweet in the reddening, dusty late-day sunlight as soft music, he heard it, and pulled back hard from his thoughts to look, to concentrate on the girl coming up the slope to his right, over on the same old trail Emilio Sanchez had used.

Maria Peralta.

The soul of Juan Valdez stirred for the first time this day. The soul of Charles Southcott-Juan Valdez.

She came slowly but with a lithe suppleness as though climbing to the foothills was easy for her. The slowness seemed to be connected with the faintly vexed expression she wore.

Her hair was thick and raven-black. It hung in waved ripples, to her shoulders, which were round and full, like her breasts, visible in full form and outlined through the cotton blouse. She was long-legged. Charles Southcott remembered her very well, although three years earlier he had only glimpsed her briefly, walking through the soft November afternoon hand-in-hand with the young man—with Juan Valdez, except that he had hardly heeded the young man that other time.

Not often in a man's lifetime, perhaps no more than once in the life of most men, a woman or a girl appeared briefly, then was forever lost, who lingered ever after in a man's memory, and regardless of how many years passed, she always appeared the same, in recollection, young and beautiful and pure, a catalyst between what *should* have been and what never was. Maria Peralta was that woman to Charles Southcott. Dream or not, he finally found the one thing he did not want changed; the one thing from which he did not

87

want to depart, if there was to be an awakening.

CHAPTER TEN

THE SIGN OF THE MOON

Maria Peralta's disposition was a product of equal parts heritage and environment. Her philosophy was a blending of things taught and endured and if it lacked anything, it was originality.

She understood perfectly *who* she was and *what* she was.

She could have left the village four years earlier when she had been eighteen, with her friend Francesca Yrigoyen, but something told her to stay, that her place was at Villa Real; it had also told her what her destiny was to be, and all this had come about when she had first noticed Juan Valdez and he had first noticed her. A year later nothing short of a Vision could have made her leave, and even had the Glorious Lady come as She occasionally did to young girls, commonly in the tan-turned arroyos of the mountainsides, to instruct Maria Peralta in her duty as a novice of God, telling her to leave the village, Maria Peralta could only have gone away providing Juan Valdez would depart with her.

There had been no Vision and Father Francisco Ordoñez had married them, and now for two additional years she had been a man's comfort and his solace, which was exactly what she had known from budding girlhood was her purpose.

Even when, as upon this day, Juan Valdez over-slept on the mountainslope, which did not happen too often but which vexed her when it did occur, she could not continue to be annoyed for two reasons; one was that Maria's temper could flash white-hot in a scalding moment, then it burnt to ash in seconds. The other reason, as she saw Juan watching her coming to him up the trail, was simply that she loved him with a fulfillment that pushed away all other sentiments.

Old Sanchez, down at the upper end of the village had smiled when he'd said her man was asleep amid his animals under a tree up the slope. She had been standing outside the little rock-and-mortar house, hand protecting her eyes, looking far outward and upward for the dust Juan made with the flock when he came towards home. There had been no sign of him, Emilio had come along, and after that Maria had started out.

This afternoon when she came to him, he did not smile as he usually did, and such was the knowledge of a woman that she could feel the meaning behind a man's gaze. Juan's steady, pensive expression had its clear meaning, but ordinarily when he looked at her like this, with his eyes half-hooded, and his gentle mouth softened away from all resolve, the tenderness was more marked.

She toiled the last few yards then halted and put both hands upon her hips. 'You over-slept, so I came to waken you.'

He nodded without moving. 'Maria,' he murmured, and marvelled at the way red sunset caught and dully flamed in her midnight hair. 'You are beautiful.'

She sighed. 'Juan.'

'Well; you are.' It was true; with failing daylight flashing its last brilliance outward and downward, she stood erect and strong, unhampered by any of the elastic aids city-women wore under their dresses, firm and fully round and muscular. Since she had been noticeable to Juan Valdez, Maria Peralta had only to pass by in the village and raise her eyes to him from a distance, and there had been an instantaneous communication between them that reached over the heads of all others to touch his heart and mind.

She laughed self-consciously. 'Well; are you going to sit and just stare?'

He responded with a quick-flashing smile. 'No. Come up and sit here by me.'

Her eyes twinkled knowledgeably. 'No. Not here. Look; the flock is going home without you. Now come along.'

It was true, the goats were leading, as

always, and the sheep followed after in dumb-brute fashion. They were raising a small dust on the descent. He said, 'Let them go. This is a very pleasant spot, isn't it?'

She knew exactly what he meant by that. She had spent an early evening at this place with him over two years ago, and if she had not torn free they would never have left until perhaps long after the moon had risen. She turned to avoid his eyes, saying, 'Come along,' and started back down. He arose and followed, half in resignation, half in anticipation. Being a man had its hells and its heavens.

The animals, motivated by thirst as much as by their homing instincts, lined out, the goats leading, once they reached the trail, and far back Juan walked with Maria.

She said, 'There were tourists in the village again, this afternoon. English, I think. They seem more pink than the others, and less comprehensible the way they stand and look, but without wanting to appear to be looking.'

Tourists meant little to him, except that they usually made him vaguely wonder how they managed to have the money to travel. He had never been to Valencia, although once, with two other men, he had visited Barcelona, and had been un-manned by the experience.

'Emilio Sanchez told me once that they are always at war with someone,' he said, absently, watching the power and sweep of her lithe stride.

She looked up. 'No. That was the Germans. I remember.'

He shrugged. Germans, English, what was the difference? He raised his eyes and watched up ahead to see which goat would finally take the lead. If it was Hernan' with the brown-stained whiskers and the amber eyes, why then the flock would turn right at the outskirts of town and march properly into the stone pen. Hernan' was almost a man. If it was scatterbrained Flacco, why then the flock would mill and bleat, and wander on past until someone shooed them back with a waving apron or a threatening faggot.

It was Hernan'. Juan turned back to his previous thoughts. 'There is a full moon tonight.'

Maria blushed. 'You know what Father Ordoñez says about that kind of thing. Pagan superstition. A woman conceives according to the will of God, and also if her body is ready. Otherwise regardless of the sign of the moon, or the arrangement of the star-signs, she does not.' Maria turned her head quickly. 'Sometimes I could die over your disappointment.'

He smiled. 'I've told you, it's all right. In time, in time, and meanwhile ...' He kept smiling down into her soft-sweet face.

She took his hand and clung to the fingers, and up ahead the lead-goat turned properly and led his four-footed brigade into the stone

92

pen where they all surrounded the trough and drank, and paused a bit, then resumed drinking, with much bumping and shoving and complaining.

When the ewes lambed it meant money; when the she-goats dropped young it meant meat for the household as well as milk and cheese. The division was about equal in interest, for while the goats brought in far less money than the sheep, they sustained Juan and Maria, and that was as important as the income derived twice a year from wool and butcher-lambs.

When Maria closed the gate the animals were already beginning to seek their places within the large enclosure. Beyond, where the citrus and olive trees stood in uneven ranks— they had once been in even ranks, but old trees succumbed to boring beetles and blight, eventually—a spindrift of thin dark smoke was arising from the nearest homes, and back along the mountain slope shadows were running downward with the slowness of cold oil.

The sea was lost out where two worlds, one below, one above, made a blurred merging. This particular time of day, or evening, was when a person standing in solitude and quiet, felt most deeply the agelessness of this peninsular environment. Juan Valdez liked the dawn and the dusk best. He leaned beside Maria and reached a sinewy arm round her middle, marvelling that even after two years, when he touched her the shock was equally as momentous to him now as it had been that first time.

She leaned a little, her only response, but it was enough. It was a yielding as full of promise as a man could hope for. It was also the powerful factor that could complete the blending of Charles Southcott with the gentle shepherd Juan Valdez.

Maria's tawny eyes lay wonderingly upon a she-goat that was heavy to springing. 'For the animals it seems too easy. Look at *Violeta*. This will be her seventh and she never fails.'

He tightened his grip round her waist. 'Well; she is experienced at this. Anyway, she is an animal. You heard the Old Señora say the longer people wait, the better the product.' He smiled as she laid her head upon his shoulder. It was not difficult, after a year of this, to understand how it was with Maria. A woman, if she were *really* a woman, knew her purpose and wished to vindicate herself through performing it.

On the other hand there was the will of God. For whatever reason, it would not happen until He wished for it to, and that was that.

He kissed her, then took her by the hand, not towards the house but around the pen to the shadowy place where their trees stood in the quiet dusk. This place was slightly uphill, and while there were neighbours not far distant, without daylight they might as well have been

94

alone in a secret place.

Father Ordoñez was a wise and saintly man; still, even after two thousand years there were lingering dark urges within the remembering blood, and if a man sought conception while the high, full moon bathed his body in its ghostly power and quicksilver beauty, a man's power was inordinantly enhanced.

Maria possessed the Catalonian fire, and somewhere far back—even her grandmother had not known exactly how far back—there had come into the Peraltas an infusion of Basque passion.

She did not accredit the full moon; she was orthodox. Still and all, it could only help, if there were anything to this superstition at all. But if there hadn't been anything to it she would have yielded the same way, with the full, demanding and consuming passion that sent her into a kind of ecstatic oblivion, because as the good God knew, Juan's touch was irresistible.

It had been such an age of time for him, such a prolonged epoch of endurance and deprivation, that he had almost forgot what this could be like. For a weak man it was the one variety of voluptuous perfection he could lose himself in, forgetting everything else. For a strong man it was the apex of sweet violence, a distinct kind of triumph and masculine dominance.

But for a combination weak and strong

95

man, it was bliss that mauled the soul and drained dry the longing spirit. Charles Southcott sublimated himself in the ethos of Juan Valdez without equivocation, accepting all the ridiculous earthy things as of total relevance to life and destiny. Even the full moon and the hushed night and the soft angelus made by silent tree-leaves overhead that seemed to sing without sound, filled him with an old-new concept of what had meaning in life.

Afterwards he lay beside her as weak as a kitten watching through a pattern of leaves the majestic trajectory of that great moon which in Boston, Massachusetts, meant only that another month had passed since men had walked up there, destroying something as old as Time by their profanations.

'Juan...?'

He lifted himself with a great effort and leaned to look. She was the kind of sweet-tender sight that choked off a man's breath in mid-sweep. He brushed her heavy mouth then pulled back.

'I am here.'

'You—were different.'

He understood, and felt a troubled sadness. 'Yes.'

She smiled upwards from the depth of her dark eyes with the shadow of her soul showing clearly. 'This time God will be good, I know it, Juan.'

He smiled. 'I know it, too.' He touched her golden throat and realised without thinking about it at all, that whatever Doctor Whalen had done, Charles Southcott did not ever want un-done.

She heaved an unsteady sigh. 'I don't even know how to begin to tell you of all the ways I love you, Juan.'

'Just love me,' he said, and let his hand glide lower until he could feel the strong, youthful beat of her heart in its velvet valley.

She stirred languidly. 'I don't want to leave.'

'No need.'

'Yes there is.' She loosened all over, though, and did not make the effort again for a little while. 'Supper,' she said drowsily. 'The work yet to be done.' She smiled, the gradual return of reality bringing her back down to habit and custom and tradition. 'Help me up.'

He shook his head. 'No. This is a special time for us. Help me make it last.'

She continued to smile. 'Yes. All right then, but in the morning don't scold.' She raised her bare arms to his shoulders.

CHAPTER ELEVEN

WHALEN'S DISASTER

At first there was no reason for anxiety because the patient reacted to sedation as normally as

97

other patients reacted, but by evening of the day after his heart surgery, the patient's languor began to cause some worry. When Walter Whalen left Boston General shortly before five o'clock the first stirrings of dread rode his spirit. He had said nothing, though, even when Leon Swansinger had been called to a conference with John Ames and Ronald Hammond.

It had been Chief Night Resident Hammond who had first begun to suspect Charles Southcott was not responding even when the sedation was allowed to wear off. Hammond had called Ames first, then Walter Whalen, and finally, by evening of that day following surgery, the full conference had been convened.

Uniquely, John Ames had been very kind towards Walter Whalen. After two hours of tests had been analysed Ames had said, in the staff room, that physically, Charles Southcott was progressing better than any post-operative patient of heart surgery he had ever seen. *Physically.* But there appeared to be something out of kilter in his consciousness. He talked, and moved his head and eyes, and performed most bodily functions as functionally, as instinctively, as anyone could expect, and yet his answers, his dull eyes, his foggy responses to any question requiring more than an instinctual reply, hinted at some kind of mental stoppage.

John Ames did not carry this statement to the logical conclusion: that Doctor Whalen's innovation was responsible. Instead, he put forth the suggestion that a psychiatric team be brought in. He also put forth the suggestion that none of this should be discussed beyond the walls of the conference room.

To this latter notion Leon Swansinger, who refused to look at Walter Whalen throughout the meeting, said, 'Just how, exactly, is Southcott's wife to be kept in the dark? And his attorney, who drew up those non-responsibility papers? They'll be around. I'm surprised they haven't been around already. What will *their* reaction be to the information that while we've accomplished our surgical purpose—we have created a mental vegetable?'

The meeting had lasted another half hour after Swansinger's candid outburst, and had ended with everyone concurring with John Ames's suggestion that a psychiatric team be brought in. On the way out none of the others had looked at Doctor Whalen, but John Ames put a hand on Walter's shoulder to detain him, and when they had been alone in the room, John Ames had said, 'Walter, whatever has happened, you are the only one with enough insight into the function of the cause—at least what appears to be the cause—to supply an answer or, more hopefully, a remedy.'

Whalen had stood there shaking his head.

He was completely at a loss, and now, leaving the hospital on a bleak, clear November night, he felt too numb to think.

He drove home in a mental fog, and even after this wore off he was still floundering. He had no idea what had happened, or *how* it happened, but with a highball in hand and some measure of control, eventually, he began to wonder if what he hadn't done to all those animals was this same thing.

He had, he reasoned, been working with experimental creatures with which he—nor anyone else—could communicate. They had been the so-called 'dumb' animals, and since they all functioned primarily by instinct to begin with, if he had done the same thing to them that his innovation had evidently done to Charles Southcott, there was no way for him to know it.

This ameliorated nothing. It amounted to no more than a theory, and even if he could prove it to be true, he would still have no idea about how it had come about, nor how to remedy it.

Swansinger's remark about Mrs Southcott and the attorney made his stomach ball up into a hard knot. Regardless of those responsibility waivers, she, and the lawyers, would certainly take Walter Whalen, and probably Boston General Hospital, to court.

If it could be proved that Whalen's device had been used on Charles Southcott without sufficient experimentation, if Doctor Whalen had preyed upon Southcott's ignorance of medical matters to persuade Southcott to allow Doctor Whalen to try the innovation on him, then all the non-responsibility waivers under the sun were not going to prevent Whalen and Boston General from being sued to the hilt, and probably adjudged accountable. Which could very easily mean bankruptcy for Walter Whalen and something nearly as disastrous for Boston General.

Walter finished the drink and returned to the bar for a second one, but before he tasted it he left the glass atop the bar and went to his laboratory. His innovation was sitting atop the table where he had put it upon returning from the hospital. He removed it from the case and stood dumbly staring at it. What he had evidently done was develop a blind spot, in himself, concerning the actual matter of creating, and sustaining, unconsciousness. Which meant that he had lifted out the awareness, which was the precise purpose of the invention, without considering what might happen to it after it was divorced from the body. He had been so positive of success he had completely overlooked the fact that consciousness in a reasoning animal—man— had to be different from the consciousness in an unreasoning creature—animal.

Whatever the psychiatrists might reveal, and Walter thought he knew what that was going to be; Swansinger had said it—vegetablism—

the baffling part of all this was *where* Charles Southcott's divorced awareness was, and how had it got there, and how in the name of God it could be got back.

Walter considered a fresh series of experiments. But since these would have to be conducted on animals, again, it was highly unlikely that they would solve the riddle of the reasoning creature's consciousness. What he really needed was another human guinea-pig, and that was not going to be easy to get. Not now. Even if he could find a volunteer willing, for a large sum of money, to undergo a test with the machine, if John Ames or anyone else connected with the local, or national, medical association, got wind of what he was trying, they would certainly get a court injunction to keep him from doing to someone else what he had done to Charles Southcott.

Sooner or later there was going to be notoriety. A thing like this was what newspapers thrived upon. They would pillory Walter Whalen from one end of the country to the other. In fact, since the news services lived off one another, the notoriety would become world-wide in a matter of days.

Walter rather listlessly plugged in the box and turned the knob until the headband, which was lying upon the table close at hand, was emanting its silent force of mind-changing decibels. It was a pointless thing to do, but somewhere within this thing, as it was now functioning harmlessly upon the table, was the answer as to what had happened to Charles Southcott.

Whalen leaned on the table watching the box and the empty headband. What he had evidently done was become involved in some vast mystery having to do with human consciousness of which he had no knowledge, and which was apparently very delicate and complicated. In a way, it was not unlike lifting the soul from a human body.

What he had done was completely liberate a human psyche. He had separated not just consciousness from the instinctive mind of a human animal, he had completely liberated it from whatever ties ordinarily held it bound to an individual intelligence.

The idea made him want to groan aloud. There was no one on earth who would be able to help him. There was no one who had ever proved, and not very many who had ever even theorised, that consciousness, intelligence, and psyche, were integrated; that when a rational creature exerted his capability for reasoning and sequential thought, it was not done by intelligence alone. Yet this was exactly what was going to be proved, if those psychiatrists came up with a finding that Charles Southcott, lying supine and helpless in his hospital bed, had been robbed of his reasoning creativity, because Southcott was still healthy, and was still capable of instinctive reaction. What he no longer possessed was independent reasoning ability nor its counterpart, the powerful character which had, coupled with his reasoning, made him uniquely Charles Southcott. In other words, what was missing was his psyche. Walter's invention had not lifted out only the consciousness—which was apparently interrelated to Southcott's integrated reason-character factor—it had lifted out Southcott's total uniqueness, his most peculiar and personal possession, his psyche.

No one knew what a psyche actually was. The fact that Walter's discovery might prove that it was an inseparable adjunct to reason and character was all well and good, but this was not going to help Walter Whalen one damned bit. He would much prefer having Charles Southcott back as he had been prior to surgery, to being remembered as the man who proved that not only was there such a thing as a psyche, but that it was inseparable from intelligence and consciousness.

Walter pulled the plug and returned to the bar for his highball, and a little later, like a drugged person, he went through the routine of showering and preparing for bed. He had not eaten. It was not that he'd forgotten dinner, it was simply that he had no appetite.

The following morning he felt little different. Except that the trauma had passed, the stunned sensation that had followed the discovery of what he had done to Southcott, was now superceded by a frantic worry, he did not feel much different from the way he had felt last night.

The shock that had paralysed his thinking processes had been replaced by a riddle that rattled round inside his head.

He was thoroughly familiar with the processes of experimentation. They were governed by sequences and precedents. When an experiment failed, the researcher went back and analysed each step, correcting, changing, altering this or that, then carrying forward again.

That was the riddle. Walter Whalen had no idea where his innovation had gone wrong. He drove to Boston General deep in thought, and upon arriving there went at once to John Ames's office.

Ames had only just arrived also. He shot Walter a look while he shed his suit coat in favour of his fresh cotton jacket and said, 'The psychiatrists were here last night.'

Walter was mildly surprised. 'Last night? I thought they'd be round this morning.'

Ames repeated it. 'Last night.' He adjusted the jacket and went after a cup of coffee. 'What I'm obsessed with,' he explained, his back to Doctor Whalen, 'is time, Walter. I don't want any delay in the Southcott matter at all. For all our sakes I want this thing resolved within the next twenty-four hours.' He lifted the cup and tasted his coffee, then paced over behind his desk. 'We won't be able to keep it quiet after that. Right now we are protected because Southcott is in Intensive Care, where no outsiders can visit him.' Ames gestured towards the coffee urn. 'Help yourself.' Whalen obeyed, and as he did so Doctor Ames kept looking at him. 'Would you like to know what the psychiatric report says, Walter?'

Whalen nodded woodenly while filling his coffee cup.

'To start with, Southcott is not as Swansinger said, a vegetable. He is more like someone who has had a coronary, and whose mind has been damaged through oxygen deprivation. What we won't know for a while yet is just how much damage there has been, and whether he can recover to any accountable degree.'

Whalen turned holding his coffee cup. He and Doctor Ames looked steadily at one another with Whalen saying nothing.

'The psychiatrists are of the opinion that your decibel-system, or whatever you choose to call it, either numbed or destroyed, or somehow or other cauterised Southcott's character-sensory-personality essence; either peeled it right out of his mind or killed it.'

'His psyche,' said Walter Whalen, meeting Ames's stony look.

Ames nodded. 'All right, his psyche. Walter, no one knows what these things are. Do you

106

understand what that means? How in God's name can we create a reversion? We don't even know what's happened.'

Whalen heard the shrillness beginning to come into Ames's voice as he said, 'What else did they say? John, I've got to have some idea where to begin.'

Ames sank down at the desk and put his coffee cup aside. 'What the hell *could* they say, Walter? They don't know much more than we know, and that's just about ground-zero. They thought Southcott's case was in some ways similar to amnesia. The reason they thought this, was because of his reaction to their other tests. But hell's bells, amnesia can be anything from the result of a blow on the head to a sudden total mental rejection of reality, and that's no help at all.'

Whalen moved to a chair and eased down. 'John, I'll tell you frankly what I think has happened is that, somehow, my innovation, which I know divorces consciousness from physical reality, has put Southcott's psyche in limbo; has set it entirely free from his body. It also seems to me that the human psyche must be tenuously, perhaps, but nevertheless relatedly integrated with intelligence, reasoning ability, and character.'

Ames threw himself back in his chair. 'What in the hell does that mean?'

Whalen was not too sure himself. 'Let's call it amnesia, for the time being. I've got to work

107

from *some* hypothesis, so I'll start from there.'

Ames gazed at Whalen and said, 'Walter; you have twenty-four hours.'

CHAPTER TWELVE

COME BACK FROM WHERE?

Amnesia, actually, was not the proper term and Walter Whalen knew it wasn't. Amnesia meant a loss of memory. It was a general term, not a specific one, and therefore it did not really fit the Southcott case at all. Being amnesic was rather like suffering from colic; it simply implied an abnormality, not a specific ailment, and could be used to cover just about anything that constituted a physical malfunction. Amnesia could be used to describe someone's inability to recall a dream, or their inability to recall their name.

Walter Whalen was not a psychiatrist, nor did he feel that psychiatry, which was another broad and general term meaning simply the study of mental and nervous disorders, would supply much in the way of worthwhile answers.

On the other hand it was the only field related to Walter's speciality, medicine, that even suggested a possibility. After all, the designation psychiatry *was* derived from the

Greek word *psyche*, meaning the relationship between mind, soul, and character.

Walter had a friend who was a competent psychiatrist, but he chose not to consult him. Not yet. Perhaps later, if he could not find his way through the mystery by himself.

He was at lunch when a fragment from his conversation with John Ames fused with an errant thought of his own. John had told him that the psychiatric team had reported how Southcott had reacted blankly to a picture of Margaret Southcott. He did not know her, his own wife of many years. What that seemed to prove was that Southcott's psyche was connected in some way to Southcott's memory bank. On other subjects the psychiatrists had reported that Southcott responded, but vaguely, indifferently, to matters requiring at least a small measure of recall.

So—Southcott's memory bank seemed to have lost its total recall in a particular way, only. Why would a man be completely unable to recognise a woman he had lived with at least half his lifetime? *Because this was something he subconsciously wished not to remember.*

Walter left the restaurant, returned to Boston General, strode down the hall to his office ignoring the looks he got, and dialled Philip Bourdon, the society doctor. The moment he identified himself Doctor Bourdon wanted to know how Charles Southcott was coming along. Walter did not have to lie.

'The surgery was a success, but of course he'll be in Intensive Care for a few more days.'

Bourdon sounded pleased. 'I'm glad to hear it. Men like that aren't easily replaced.'

Whalen had a sardonic thought: men like Southcott were indeed hard to replace where society doctors were concerned. But that was just a thought. What Whalen had in mind was a question.

'Tell me, Doctor, between the two of us, do the Southcotts get along well, or not?'

Bourdon was slow to answer. It was a question, in fact, that he would not normally have answered at all. But Walter Whalen was a respected man in his field; it would be safe to assume he would not have asked this question if he did not have an excellent reason for doing so. Philip Bourdon said, 'You know how it is, Doctor Whalen. Couples, particularly if the brainy part is successful, tend to grow apart. I hear gossip all day long about couples doing this . . . I would say no, that the Southcotts have been drifting farther and farther apart for a number of years, that they do not really have the old affinity any more. But then, who does?' Doctor Bourdon chuckled, and Walter Whalen chuckled right along with him. Then Walter asked his next question.

'By any chance, Doctor, is there any gossip about Charles Southcott?'

Bourdon said, 'Women? No, I'm sure there's not. I'd have heard it, surely, if there were. On

110

the other hand, Whalen, Mister Southcott occasionally goes abroad on business. You know as well as I do what opportunities that sort of thing presents. A couple of years ago— three, I think—he went off to France and was gone for several weeks. His wife told me of this.'

'She was suspicious, perhaps?'

Bourdon did not think so. 'I didn't get that impression, no. But she *did* tell me that he was getting harder for her to control.'

Walter had enough and rang off. Hard to control? A man like Charles Southcott controlled by a woman? Impossible. *But*—if a woman tried to dominate a man like Southcott, he would most certainly resent it.

Walter arose from the desk and went to stand by the window. Charles Southcott did not like Margaret Southcott. His kind of a man either divorced a woman, or threw himself into a compensatory outlet, but in either case, given a valid excuse *he would willingly forget her.*

Walter Whalen's innovation had provided Charles Southcott with the most genuinely valid excuse imaginable!

Walter felt the first thrill of encouragement since the discovery that his innovation had all but destroyed a man. But he admonished himself to be cautious, to be secretive.

He went up to the staff room and got a cup of coffee and returned with it to his office, just in time to answer a telephone call from John

111

Ames. In order that Walter would have every opportunity to do whatever he could, Ames had arranged for his rounds to be made by other members of staff.

Walter thanked Ames and rang off. He had been tempted to mention his conversation with Philip Bourdon, but at the last moment had decided to heed caution. There was no point in saying anything. Perhaps it did not really mean anything. Perhaps Walter was striving so hard to find a basis for his current pursuit that he was attaching significance where it was not deserved.

But this was *all* he had. He finished the coffee and tried to imagine how to utilise the scrap of information he had. Southcott had been willing to forget his wife, and he had done it more completely than he had forgotten other things. Fine. But what of it? What Walter needed was not some scrap of intelligence out of context, what he needed was...

Very slowly he turned from the window. All feelings had compensatory corollaries. When a normal man could no longer stand his wife, providing he was healthy, virile, and not unduly introverted, he found a compensation.

But Bourdon had said there was no scandal connected with Charles Southcott's name ... he had also said something about the opportunities available to businessmen travelling alone overseas.

Walter went back to the desk and sat down

112

again. The intriguing aspect of this kind of reasoning was that it could, possibly, lead him to some girl in Europe with whom Southcott had had a *liaison*, but what in the hell good would locating the woman or verifying the *liaison* do now? What he had to deal with was not a physical matter at all, it was so altogether different that he could not even give it a proper name.

But he could not put the matter of the connection between Southcott's total rejection of his wife, and the fact of normal compensation, out of his mind. Eventually, he went along to the Intensive Care unit and visited Southcott. The private nurse was there, as statuesque as ever. She made such a painful effort to keep any expression from showing it embarrassed Walter Whalen.

To establish *something* between them, he asked how the healing process was coming along. The nurse said it was entirely satisfactory. When Walter approached the still, burly figure on the bed, the nurse stepped to the opposite side of the bed, giving Walter the impression that she had either been instructed what to do if Doctor Whalen came round, or else that she had already decided what to do, on her own, if he arrived. Walter smiled across at her; he had never before felt the way he did now, as though he were a vampire come to fasten upon the jugular of a helpless victim.

113

He asked Southcott how he felt, and got only a flicker of eyelids to indicate that he had even been heard. He felt Southcott's pulse and found it strong and proper. He studied his face, his eyes, the slackness of the mouth, and asked if Southcott were hungry. This time he got a little negative head-shake, which was a start in the right direction. He asked if Southcott wished for anything, and again the eyelids flickered but there was neither a negative nor an affirmative answer.

Walter went back to basic things, asking if Southcott were cold. The answer was another negative head-shake. He asked if Southcott were thirsty, and again got the head-shake.

This, of course, confirmed only what the psychiatric team had already reported; that Charles Southcott could respond correctly to questions related to instinctive things, and that he could not relate to things that required a more sophisticated thought-process, as when Walter had asked if Southcott wanted anything in particular.

The statuesque nurse said, 'Doctor, this is how he has been since the original sedation wore off. You thought he might move or be restless. Well; you see him now as he has been since they brought him here from surgery.'

The tone had been full of reproach, and that irritated Doctor Whalen, but he kept it to himself, thanked the nurse and went ponderously back to his office.

Was it possible that the psyche of that vegetable in Intensive Care could have relocated somewhere else, and if so, how could it be proved? He finally yielded to temptation and telephoned his friend whose speciality was psychiatry.

'This,' he told the psychiatrist, 'is going to sound insane to you, Albert, but in your handling of amnesiacs have you ever had reason to speculate about the possibility of amnesiacs going somewhere else, mentally, while they were blocked out?'

The psychiatrist was a dry, very knowledgeable man. 'What in the hell have you been reading, Walter? Go somewhere else? What does that mean?'

Walter laughed uncomfortably. 'Well; they certainly aren't *here*, are they? I mean, when a person's mind goes blank, does that necessarily mean they have simply developed a stoppage, a sort of intellectual paralysis, or could it mean that the mind, which we in medicine know for a fact never rests, just is—on a trip?'

The psychiatrist said, 'It's mid-afternoon, Walter; have you started your attitude adjustment hour this early in the day? It doesn't *go* anywhere, Walter; when there is no recall, the mind simply ceases to function. Where could it go?'

'I have no idea,' Whalen admitted. 'I'm just postulating an idea. Okay; then forget that and tell me this, Albert: what is anamnesis?'

The psychiatrist cleared his throat in the manner of a man preparing to be sententious. 'You know what it is as well as I do. A patient's account of his illness.'

'Including sensations while his is anaesthetised,' said Walter.

'Supposedly, yes, but—.'

'Wait a minute,' interrupted Whalen. 'Suppose anamnesis were to include something absolutely foreign to the patient's immediate recall, Albert. Suppose it went back in his memory a year, or five years, or maybe ten years, to something he remembered from somewhere else, or remembered from something that happened to him, or something he saw and vividly recalled: tell me this: in your profession don't you fairly often encounter this kind of irrelevant recall in people who are unable to react normally?'

'Certainly,' said the psychiatrist. 'Hallucinations and legitimate recall are common. Now let *me* ask *you* a question, Walter: are you talking about a specific patient?'

'Yes.'

'All right. Now then, does this particular patient remember something, perhaps from childhood?'

'That's it, Albert: this damned patient is blanked out on some things and not entirely on other things.'

'Okay; then what you probably have is

116

mental rejection.'

Walter agreed. 'I know that. What I'm interested in is what specifically happens when a mind is freed of these rejections, these distasteful inhibitions.'

The psychiatrist snorted. 'I'm also interested in that. So is every other head-shrinker in the business, Walter. And I suppose that someday we will know, but right now all I can suggest is that you have some experienced man take a look at your patient. Not I, because I'm so busy right now I meet myself going and coming. By the way, what is it that your patient can't recall?'

'His wife.'

The psychiatrist laughed for the first time. 'Can't say that I blame him, poor devil. But of course he'll probably have to come back and face that, won't he?'

Walter agreed and rang off. Out of this entire conversation several words from the last remark stood out: he'll probably *have to come back* and face that, won't he? That was the crux. Come back from *where*?

CHAPTER THIRTEEN

DOCTOR WHALEN'S DECISION

John Ames arrived at Walter Whalen's office a little after three o'clock, and although Ames

117

did not look quite grim, those who had seen him pacing down the corridor could tell from the set of jaw and mouth that he was not paying Doctor Whalen a purely social call.

Walter was on the telephone. He motioned Ames in from the doorway and pointed to a chair opposite the desk and near the rear-wall window. Ames dutifully went over, sat, then turned to stare out into the early-settling wintertime dusk.

Walter had a large, lined, yellow tablet on the desk and from time to time he added a notation to the numbered paragraphs there, then he completed his call and put the telephone down, dropped his pen and looked up.

Ames said, 'It'll sound trite if I ask whether you've come up with anything, won't it?'

Walter looked at the scribbling in front of him before replying. 'It might, and I'll have to answer by saying that I've learned an awful lot about Charles Southcott today, all the way from his college days to his business successes, to his over-the-years increasing antipathy for Mrs Southcott.'

Ames was not only unimpressed, he evidently was annoyed. 'Walter, it was *his wife* that inspired this visit. She dropped by this afternoon. I took her to Intensive Care and let her look in, then I got her out of there. She said he looked remarkably well.' John Ames

118

crossed one leg over the other one. 'And he does, for a fact, look well . . . she will be back in another couple of days. How do we handle her then?'

Whalen did not know, but he did what anyone might have done in his place, he played for time. 'Two days can be a long while, John.'

Ames did not accept that at all. 'Two days can be all any of us will need to go down the tube, Walter. Have you come up with anything?'

'If you mean, do I know how to perhaps reverse the innovative effect, the answer is no, I do not know how to do that. If you mean, have I made any progress in defining, or probing what happened . . . I think I may have made a little. A very little, John.'

Ames did not show encouragement. 'In what way?'

Walter retreated. 'A theory only.'

Ames flushed. 'A theory. Walter, gawddammit, we don't have the time for that. It's a luxury we simply cannot afford. I meant it when I said you had twenty-four hours. After that, there simply will have to be some positive kind of statement issued about Mister Southcott's condition. We've already said he is making progress and appears to be well on the way, which is the standard release, as you know. Even if we could exclude the press, which we can't, not with someone as prominent as Charles Southcott, we'd still

119

have to do better than just the routine "he is making progress" statement, to his wife if to no one else.' Ames drew back a breath before continuing. 'We can't keep him in Intensive Care indefinitely, and if we try it, it will be the same as saying something has gone wrong. Twenty-four hours from this morning. Walter; you can't rest on a theory.'

Whalen had never intended to rest on it, but he was unable to pull a rabbit out of a hat, and whether John Ames agreed or approved, or did neither of those things, the fact remained that there was absolutely no short-cut; not in this affair where every step was no more than an inch at a time, and every guess had to be verified and re-verified.

Whalen sat hunched, gazing at John Ames. There was no way to make Ames understand, now, any more than there had been before, when Walter Whalen had been so positive about his innovation. All Ames was concerned with was success. Well; that was all Whalen wanted, too, but even in a case of childhood measles, the cure took time. The trouble was that to mention some such examples as this was not going to change John Ames and it was not going to change Whalen's unique dilemma. He had twenty-four hours. Regardless of whether he needed forty-eight or a hundred-and-eight, he had twenty-four.

There was another reason why Walter Whalen sat for a long time in silence: he was

120

gong to fly out of Boston International Airport at six o'clock this evening for Europe. Specifically for France, and if he told Ames that, and tried to explain *why* he was going to do it, Ames would explode.

In fact, Ames might even get a restraining order to prohibit Whalen from leaving the United States. No matter how reasonable Whalen's reason might sound—and, actually, it wouldn't really sound reasonable at all, it would sound mystifyingly far out—Ames would not think of the reason, he would think of Whalen leaving, and of John Ames and Boston General being left to hold the sack when it finally got out what had happened to Charles Southcott.

Finally, Whalen said, 'John, I'm doing everything humanly possible, and you surely must realise that.'

Ames softened a little. 'Yes, of course.' He even levered up a little smile at Walter Whalen. 'But I wish to gawd you'd listened to me, Walter.'

Whalen returned the smile, wryly. 'So do I—now. But I still have all day tomorrow, haven't I?'

Ames allowed the smile to die. 'Yes, but I can't help feeling damned helpless. Well; about this theory of yours...'

Whalen leaned back off the desk making up his mind then and there that he was not going to explain his theory to John Ames, the

121

eminent medical practitioner who had no imagination, and who also had absolutely no sympathy for things Walter had heard him denounce as fraud because they did not derive from basic biology.

Walter tried temporising. 'I'm going to work on it tonight, trying to reduce some tangents to medical denominators. Essentially, the theory has to do with the possibility that somehow, Southcott's psyche has retrogressed.'

Ames's face wrinkled. 'Has what?'

'Well; Southcott's psyche has been thoroughly separated from him, and has re-settled somewhere else; probably in some area where he has total recall. In memory, in other words.' Whalen tried to smile against the gradual hostility he saw forming over by the rear-wall window. 'John, I've verified the possibility of such a thing through Albert Hardesty, President of the Massachusetts Institute of Psychiatry.'

Ames said, 'Occultism, Walter. Gawddamned occultism. I'll tell you right now, that if you have some idea of using that confounded device of yours in reverse, or something like that, in any crazy scheme to bring back Southcott's psyche, this time I'll stop you by force, if I have to.'

Walter Whalen spoke softly, soothingly. 'My innovation is entirely out of it, John.' He had not intended to reveal as much as he had, but it was difficult to start explaining even the

122

rudiments of a theory, and not present some kind of continuity or conclusion.

Ames's hostility lingered, but not altogether openly. He said, 'Regardless, Walter, I don't believe you can do it. My impression is that you don't know any more now than you knew yesterday.' Ames arose as though to depart. 'I've got a statement drawn up on my desk you may want to glance at before you leave tonight, Walter. It's an explanation of what we'll have to tell the press. I'm sending it over to the directors in the morning.' Ames went to the door and leaned there. 'I'm thinking in terms of defence, which is really all that I can do. Not only defence of myself, but of Boston General ... Walter, you don't look so good in what I could not keep out of the statement to the directorship. I'm sorry. I'm truly and sincerely sorry, Walter, but what else can I do?'

John Ames departed. Doctor Whalen watched the door close, and leaned ahead to clasp both hands atop the desk. Whether his idea about Charles Southcott was right or wrong, Walter Whalen MD was finished as a practising physician. Win, lose or draw, he was finished. Even if he succeeded in bringing Southcott and his errant psyche together again, he was still finished.

A man did not have to possess perspicacity in large doses to realise the kind of suspicion and mistrust that would accrue to his name once the newspapers started making a Roman holiday out of the kind of strange, far-out thing Walter Whalen had done.

To make matters worse, if Ames or the directors, or the news services, or just the local staff at Boston General, knew what was in Walter Whalen's mind right at this moment, one of them, probably the press, would start up a great clamour for Walter Whalen to be committed; would set up a hue and cry to have him restricted and subjected to psychiatric examinations to prove he was insane.

He was almost ready to accept some such hypothesis himself. Any presumably sane man, trained in the black-and-white world of medical fact, who actually entertained some idea that he could find another person's misplaced psyche could hardly be normal. Even to himself.

Walter put on his street-coat, doused the light on his desk, gathered his notes and stuffed them into a pocket as he left the office. Up the corridor at the Nurse's Station, the usual cluster of nurses, orderlies, X-ray and other technicians were crowding in to share coffee and gossip before shift-change. Walter winced at the prospect of marching past that throng, but it had to be done. He could guess that they had already gossiped about his involvement with the Southcott case, and had passed their judgements.

It had to be quite wonderful to be a lifelong mediocrity; that way a person was never upon

124

a pedestal where other, routinely small and narrow, people, could snipe and derogate and vindictively seek to tear one down. Walter went past the Nurse's Station conscious that the talk had nearly ceased, as every head turned to watch his progress.

When he reached the front of the building, up where Administration was, young Spencer Littleton came swiftly out a door and almost collided with Doctor Whalen. Spencer stammered his profuse apology, then, as he recognised Walter, the apologies began to dwindle.

Walter smiled as though he had seen no shadow swiftly come and go upon the younger man's face. 'It was nothing. I've been trampled worse in uptown lifts.'

Doctor Littleton fell in beside Doctor Whalen and, head down, walked on through towards the massive and electrically-operated front doors as though wishing not to be recognised. As they emerged into the early night though, Spencer Littleton said, 'It's going to be one hell of a mess, Doctor Whalen. Everyone's talking about it. I wish there was something I could do.'

Whalen was touched. Littleton was a sincere person; he had meant that just as he had said it. Then he said something that had a different ring to it.

'One of the people will undoubtedly try to sell the secret to a newspaper by tomorrow,

125

Doctor Whalen. All it'll require will be for the right person to eventually pick up the story as it goes round the hospital.'

Littleton smiled, ducked his head against the cold, and went swiftly in the direction of the parking area.

Walter roused himself, studied his watch, then also hurried along. He had plenty of time, but still and all when a man owned a large home he did not just fill an overnighter and take a taxi to the airport the way an apartment-dweller would do.

At home, he thought a long while about leaving a note to be delivered to John Ames in the morning. He only abandoned the thought when it occurred to him that he could telephone John from France, or at least from somewhere in Europe.

Then he methodically went round making certain all his windows were securely fastened, the rear and patio doors were also secured, and finally he went to pack a suitcase.

This was the first long trip he had even considered, since serving in the navy a good many years back, and as a matter of fact he had never before actually been to Europe. He had seen it falling astern from the Mediterranean—and it hadn't inspired any vague stirrings of nostalgia or affinity—while aboard a warship, but this would be his first time there to set foot ashore.

That thought only very fleetingly occurred

to him. He was vastly more concerned with why he was going, and although he also speculated about what he might discover, or might *not* discover, what seemed most notable of all was the positively insane idea that he was clinging to.

The only reason he clung to it was because there simply was nothing else that even approached his problem, in the vaguest terms. Probably this solution only appeared to be one, but anything at all was better than sitting back there at Boston General for the next twenty or so hours, waiting for the damned bloody axe to fall.

He telephoned for a cab, then went out front in the cold and starlit night to wait for it, with his luggage. When he raised his eyes to the heavens it was as though only he and they belonged in the unrealistic travesty that his orderly life had suddenly become. Only he and they—and perhaps, somewhere in Europe, another person about whom Walter Whalen knew nothing at all, except that Charles Southcott had mentioned something about that person in his sleep one night very shortly after returning from Span and France three years earlier, and Southcott's wife had remembered; although she had never mentioned to her husband what he had said that night in his sleep.

CHAPTER FOURTEEN

THE SEARCH BEGINS

Walter Whalen had followed an almost irresistible course, partly, he thought as his aircraft bored ahead through the Atlantic night, because there was satisfaction in playing detective; partly because, the deeper he delved into the life-experience of Charles Southcott, the more fascinating it became, putting the parts of a successful man's past and present into focus, rather like fitting the parts of a puzzle together, and partly too, because these things tended to hide the basic truth, which was simply that Walter did not have any idea where to begin, in the matter of bringing back the misplaced psyche.

And of course he was fleeing. He had refused to even consider this idea back in Massachusetts, but the farther out over the ocean the aircraft carried him, the easier it was to face up to the fact. He was fleeing, and he was doing it under the deceptive guise of a clinician who had to re-trace the past of a patient.

It had not been very difficult to verify Southcott's itinerary on that European venture three years back. The airline reservations facility had been most cooperative. Otherwise, the *Boston Globe*, one of the more prestigious newspapers of Massachusetts, verified that Southcott's purpose for making that trip to France had been a merger between two companies in which he held controlling interest. One company had been a component manufacturing establishment related to the motor car industry, and the other company had been a motor car sales and service establishment. Merging was advisable, the *Globe*'s financial analyst had written, in the face of the variety of stiff competition the Japanese and Germans were bringing to bear.

But what had really decided Walter to embark on this trip, aside from an increasingly strong subconscious urge to run, was that remark spoken in Southcott's sleep, which his wife had remembered very well, and which she had revealed to Walter Whalen over the telephone.

'My God; Aphrodite brought to earth in the dust of Spain.'

Margaret Southcott had nursed those eleven words for three years. She recalled them for Walter in a tone of oddly detached bitterness. Walter's reaction to them had been interest blended with surprise; Charles Southcott had definitely *not* impressed Doctor Whalen as a man likely to say something poetic—except that Walter knew from experience people occasionally soared beyond their plodding

129

phlegmatism when a heartstring was touched.

This 'Aphrodite in the dust', then, was what Walter sought. His theory, based on the daylong groping at Boston General, tended to convince him that Southcott's misplaced psyche had sought about for something in Southcott's memory bank, and had settled upon this particular vivid and stirring recollection. Undoubtedly Southcott had experienced other, certainly far more recent, events, mostly having to do with his business empire or his home and Margaret, but these things became grey parts of an exisential continuity, adding to like memories down the years, while the experience in Spain had become an oasis in his secret memory bank, with a very powerful, sweet and wonderful freshness that did not fade; that, in fact, had probably grown stronger and more tantalising with the passing of time.

It was also worth speculating about that Southcott had not mentioned visiting Spain, only France. A man who hid beauty from others in order to share it with no one, did so, Walter thought, in order not to destroy a fragile and transcending experience.

But where Walter came up against a blank wall—assuming that he actually did find something—was in his conjectures of what that might be; it certainly would *not* be Charles Southcott, who was lying immobile back at Intensive Care in Boston General Hospital. He had to be philosophical about this, and a double scotch-and-soda from a stewardess helped. Moreover, thus far everything he had done towards unravelling the riddle, had been accomplished a step, or an inch, at a time. One day earlier he had not even had an inkling, and tonight he was on the track of something Charles Southcott had kept hidden, and which would probably have remained hidden if Southcott's subconscious hadn't tricked him in a dream into mentioning a girl in Spain.

If there *was* something, at the end of this trail, Walter could conceive of no way to counteract it. If the Southcott psyche had transplanted itself, Walter faced the basic fact which he had avoided facing all the previous day, and which had to be the key to his riddle: although Walter's innovation was responsible for misplacing the psyche, and he was therefore at least that much advanced over everyone else in this field, he, nor anyone else, had even a decent theory about how to detach the psyche and send it back where it originated—in the primaeval, fundamental mentality of Charles Southcott, where it had functioned in collaboration with the repetitive, instinctual animal processes, to create the civilised success that had been Charles Southcott.

He finished the highball bitterly smiling over the reaction all this would cause in his eminent friend, Albert Heinemann, the renowned psychiatrist. Someday, if he were able, Walter might look Albert up, sit him down, and explain it to him. And Albert would think he was crazy.

Maybe Albert would be correct.

Walter had a second scotch-and-soda and afterwards composed himself to sleep, in order that his psychological clock would not be hopelessly deranged when he arrived on the Continent.

But sleep eluded him, even though all around him passengers in tilted-back lounges slept like logs. He did not smoke, which would have helped, and he would have liked another drink, but controlled that urge without much effort. There was music and television, but the music flooding his mind when he adjusted the ear plugs, too strongly reminded him of how the decibels of sound had got him where he now was, and as far as the television programme was concerned, he had never been able to identify with suave detective-types who solved their complicated cases by indiscriminate shootings, while fondling beautiful women and consuming inordinate amounts of liquor.

He forced his thoughts away from the Charles Southcott affair only to have them drift back time and time again. He sought for a compromise, and eventually achieved it by thinking about John Ames.

It was impossible to recall Ames without also thinking of Boston General. One was inseparable from the other.

The inevitable, of course, since Whalen would be gone, and even if he had been there nothing would have been changed, was that within the next day or two—at the most the next four days—the sky was going to fall. Walter winced. Never, in his entire life, had he wanted to do anything like this to anyone. When the news got out, as it most certainly would and even young Spencer Littleton had been able to foresee this, Boston General was going to be thrown into a crisis that amounted to disaster. As far back as Walter could recall, no U.S. hospital had ever been involved in anything as fantastic and as unexplainable.

Regardless of how the blame was placed—on the missing Doctor Whalen— among the recriminations was surely to be the one that would substitute John Ames, because he was available, for Walter Whalen. When John defended himself, as he wold do, of course, by insisting that he had flatly refused to allow the innovation to be used, a fact he could support by the word of the staff, the logical rebuttal from the press, from Margaret Southcott, from her attornies, and from the general public, was going to be that John Amex must have been very lax, must indeed not have exerted proper control, or Walter Whalen never could have used Charles Southcott as his guinea-pig.

John would be ruined professionally. He

133

would also very probably be sued into bankruptcy by the Southcott interests.

As for the hospital, well, the building would remain, and perhaps after a year or two, with an entirely new staff, it would function again, but people would remember, and that stigma would very probably inhibit both the ill and their guardians. Boston General might, eventually, recover fully, but if this obtained, it probably would not do so for a great many years.

And as for Walter Whalen ... he changed his mind and caught a stewardess's eye to order another highball. As for Walter Whalen ... he did not know. He was a physician. That was all he wanted to be. Medicine and his speciality were all he cared about and were all he knew.

But he had destroyed himself right along with Boston General and John Ames. Back in Massachusetts he was worth, in stocks and improved real estate, roughly a half million dollars. If he tried to convert any of that, if he tried to get the converted wealth out of America, without a doubt the Commonwealth of Massachusetts, the Southcott interests, and the Federal Government as well, would launch a legal fight to have him extradited and sent home for trial.

He was not quite clear as to what charges would be brought against him: he had not murdered Southcott; technically he hadn't at any rate. Of course there was malpractice and

134

all its un-lovely off-shoots. And there was Flight to Avoid Prosecution, probably. And the illegal practice of medicine.

With the aircraft soaring unerringly and quietly through a stygian night, and with peaceful sleepers all around him, Walter stared at the off-white ceiling savouring the full measure of his disaster. He had, in a matter of one or two days, put himself in a position where everything he had been accumulating for more than twenty years, was now reduced to the money in his wallet and the clothes on his back.

The money would last quite a while; it had been his custom, unwise though this may have been, to carry large amounts of currency with him. It had become his personal measure of success after a childhood of deprivation and hardship.

But eventually the money would be spent. He lay back staring upwards; until now he had refused to face his personal predicament, but now he faced it. If not courageously, at least inevitably. The longer he lay there, semi-detached from everything else, the blacker it looked.

In the same detachment, he began to feel resentment of the man lying back there at Boston General. But that was infantile; this situation was no more the fault of Charles Southcott than it was the fault of John Ames, or smug, brisk, Leon Swansinger.

135

As he got drowsy from the heated compartment, from the soft-heard sighing of jet engines and from the stillness and hush on all sides of him, he began to have a peculiar sensation of being between two epochs in Time, the immediate past, which was back in Boston, and the future, which lay somewhere in the vicinity of the Pyrenees. He could sense the future with the same fidelity with which he could recall the past. It was a feeling of soaring above himself and looking downwards, back and ahead, and seeing a blending of Time in which the continuity was neither past nor future, but which was both of them, combined with the present. A most bizarre sensation.

He slept. The aircraft encountered turbulence, which was not unusual over the Atlantic Ocean at any time of year, but was least unusual in winter. Then it entered the vast bight lying southwesterly between Ireland and Spain, north of the Bay of Biscay, and began to lose altitude as it approached the jutting coastline of Brittany.

There was nothing visible below, for a long while. Not until Paris showed, a great sprawl of brilliance, like candles shining upwards from the interior of a honeycomb, and by then the engines were beginning to noticeably whine.

It was the pitching of his aircraft as it entered the lower atmosphere that awakened Walter Whalen. He peered from his nearside

136

porthole and saw what appeared to be a convocation of fireflies stretching in all directions to the nightbent curvings of the horizon. It was a sight never to be forgotten.

By day Paris was a patchwork of uneven rooftops and roadways that seemed to lead away, rather than towards, the heartland of the city. By night it was a combination of fretworked illogical lights, and an amphitheatre of enormous size.

The air continued bumpy all the way down to the ground. There was a cold wind blowing when the aircraft finally ran out to its limit, then waddled back to disgorge its passengers.

Even without the wind Walter would have felt more alone and adrift than he had ever felt in his life, but with that wind he felt like a buffeted autumn leaf.

The first extent of his journey—his flight from the retribution hovering over Boston General—was ended. He went through Customs like an automaton, had no difficulty in finding a taxi, and was hurtled through dark, dingy streets to a hotel. There, finally, he was able to bathe and go to bed. There too, he was finally able to finish his interrupted sleep, and although he had done nothing physical since leaving the Western Hemisphere, he felt as exhausted as someone who had been running hard for a very long while.

CHAPTER FIFTEEN

NARROWING DOWN THE SEARCH

Three years earlier Charles Southcott's itinerary had been from Paris to Lyons, and from the latter grimy metropolis to St Etienne, where the second of his companies had its manufactory.

Walter Whalen followed this identical route, and even though Southcott's itinerary presumably terminated at St Etienne, had turned back from there to Paris after a week or so, Walter Whalen knew this was not how Southcott had ended his European sojourn. He did not know, however, what route Southcott had taken from St Etienne, and evidently neither had anyone else including Margaret Southcott, the nocturnal eavesdropper, but Walter was not too worried.

As it turned out, his confidence was quite justified. An executive of the component manufactory recalled without any hesitation where Southcott had probably gone, because he had, himself, suggested it.

'To Andorra, *Monsieur*, and from there to Catalonia. It was simply because he said he was tired, and because I thought he looked tired. A week in Catalonia, *Monsieur* ... believe me, providing one avoids the great cities such as

Barcelona and Tarragona, excepting perhaps Bayonne and Biarritz, there is no place to my knowledge where a man can find such peace as in the countryside of Catalonia.'

Walter was grateful, and he was positive the Frenchman was a gentleman of such discernment that he would most certainly know the best places for relaxation. But where, exactly, had *Monsieur* Southcott gone, in Spain?

The executive had to lay a finger alongside his nose to facilitate recollection. He remembered suggesting the villages on the Ebros watershed. Places such as Mollerusa, which was actually inland, upon the Plain of Urgel, and the towns of Borjas Blancas and Espluga. But particularly, he told Walter Whalen, because he liked them best, himself, he had suggested Montblanch, and Valls and Reus, which were near the sea, and Villa Real, which lay inland a short distance and nearer the outfall of the Ebros river, a particularly enchanting place because of its serenity and antiquity, not to mention its pastels and its beautiful women, undoubtedly part Basque, with a French admixture to the Catalonian strain.

Walter departed from St Etienne in mid-afternoon with an assortment of garlic-scented people whose unending rhetoric began the moment they were aboard the public transport, and never ended, not even when the conveyance began its breathless assault of some of the most spectacular mountains Walter had ever seen, until they left the vehicle at Andorra. And he had not understood a single word of any of it.

Andorra was a fairyland. The entire world of the Pyrenees was as alien to Walter Whalen as the dark side of the moon. He could imagine a man losing himself in those mountains without any trouble, except for the fact, of course, that anyone who spoke English would be as obvious among the natives as a sore thumb.

From Andorra the scenery changed only gradually, and while the people he travelled with, on the second leg of his odyssey, seemed equally as poor and swarthy, their language sounded subtly different, and they did not appear to possess the same ebullience. Some of them, in fact, mostly older people, submitted to the unmerciful jarring and bumping with a depthless fatalism that reminded Walter of the peculiar, blank passivity of subway passengers in New York City. In both cases there seemed to be a detachment based upon resignation.

The scenery was an alternate of plains and peaks, until on the farthest slope he caught sight of the misty greenyness of the Mediterranean Sea stretching far beyond the Bay of Biscay, and as the descent quickened, he caught sight of Majorca, a hundred miles to sea from Tarragona, without knowing what it was, except that it was probably a great island.

The impression upon Walter Whalen, whose only trip of any account had been from the coalfield country of West Virginia to New England as a youth, was of being jarred and jostled and wrenched out of the Twentieth Century into the Seventeenth or Eighteenth Centuries. He had the feeling that the people he saw in their villages and upon the short-cropped, stony hillsides, who stood like statues watching him pass, were imbued with some kind of patient agelessness; were the same faces and figures that had dwelt in this hard but majestically blessed and serene world over and over again since earliest times.

The total effect was to keep him from turning inward all the way down to the sea coast, but after that, where he encountered paved roads and motor cars, lorries and motor-bikes, and where he caught the familiar smell of factories and salt-air, no different from the smell of industrial Boston, he had little trouble re-adjusting. The Mediterranean could have been the soiled Atlantic where it rose and fell along New England's industrialised shoreline.

He disembarked at Tarragona, an ancient seaport city that appeared to be a jumble of ancient and modern architecture, whose inland areas showed how the industry of hard-working agriculturists had made the soil yield an abundance of crops ranging from grapes and citrus to olives and grain, as well as livestock. The city proper had its face turned towards the sea. Walter Whalen did not have to be told that Tarragona was a very important seaport. Nor was he especially interested. What he wanted here, was a means for reaching the villages farther back against the tawny slopes, and although he probably could have hired a car and driver, he chose instead to purchase a German motorcycle, a light, but sturdy machine. It was a sanguine fact that although he heard no English spoken, as soon as he evinced interest in purchasing the motorbike, an interpreter was produced by the dealer within minutes.

Finally, near the end of day, he went back along the coast to a small hotel and got settled in for the night. Tarragona had better hotels, certainly ones with more advanced conveniences, but he chose not to remain in the city. It was bad enough—for the first time in his life—to be where he could not converse, but it was even worse to be in a place where the people seemed completely different, even from the swarthy people who lived in some sections of Boston. He chose not to be suffocated by this differentness and went back down the coast to his outlying hotel where there was more countryside to be seen, and not such an overwhelming clutter of gypsy-types.

He bought a map of the Catalonian countryside, including the provinces of

Castellon, Tarragona, and Barcelona, and at dinner that night identified each of the places the Frenchman had mentioned by their phonetic sound. He had already devised a way for locating Southcott's itinerary, and the following day experimented with this idea inland, over against the mountains, at Espluga. He offered the proprietor of the local hotel ten American dollars if he would look back in his register three years for the name Charles Southcott.

It was not listed.

The next village to be visited was Montblanch. Those other towns the Frenchman had named were even farther inland, and Walter felt certain that Charles Southcott had not gone into the highlands. He was not certain of this, but decided to play his hunch that Southcott had preferred the warmer and more beautiful Mediterranean-slope, then, if he consistently drew blanks, he could of course go deeper into the highlands.

At Montblanch he spent another ten dollars and discovered that three years ago, if an American named Charles Southcott had stopped here, at least he had not checked into a hotel.

He headed for the coast again, and at both Valls and Reus made the same offer of ten American dollars and got the same answers. Charles Southcott had not stopped in either town. At Reus, though, he learned that an

American had hired a car and driver, and the reason this was remembered was that not only were American tourists uncommon in this area, but this particular American had over-paid the man from whom he had hired the car, and who had been the American's chauffeur, twice as much as the cost of hiring the car, which was a scandalous windfall.

Walter searched out the car-owner, who spoke a little English, but not enough, actually, to comprehend half of what Walter said, although the Catalonian remembered his profligate American very well and soon as he comprehended that this was the man Walter was asking about, the Spaniard resolved everything, and reminded Walter of the adage about one picture being worth a thousand words. Particularly words in two languages that neither conversant could make head nor tails of, when they were not his own words. The car-owner produced a soiled and worn photograph of himself standing proudly beside the rich American—*all* Americans were rich—with his old car in the background.

For once, the 'rich American' appellation was correct. The man looking boldly, and a bit indulgently, out of the photograph, was definitely Charles Southcott.

Five American dollars assisted the Catalonian's memory. He had driven the rich American to several towns. He dug out a much-used map to point out the places to

Walter Whalen. They were the same towns Walter had already visited, except for two. Gandesa, which was southeasterly across the Ebro, and Villa Real, a village tucked away in a fold of some hills on the near side of the river below Mayáls a few miles.

It took a little time getting an answer to the question of whether Charles Southcott had spent the night at Gandesa or Villa Real. It turned out that he had spent the night in neither place, that he had returned to Reus and had been put up at a tiny hostel operated by a cousin of the car-owner.

No wonder the hotel people Walter had spoken to in Reus had no record of Southcott.

By the time he had managed to get the last comprehensible scrap of information from the car-owner, and had assured that enterprising Catalonian that, since he had the motor-bike, he would not wish to engage the car or its driver, it was near the end of a trying day. He declined an offer to be escorted to the little rural inn operated by his cousin, the same humble but immaculate place where the rich American, himself, had stayed three years ago, and handed over five American dollars, which the Catalonian seemed delighted to get, without using a drop of his precious petrol to earn them, and straddled the motor-bike in an undecided manner; Reus had accommodation. He could have spent the night there. On the other hand there was some kind of inn at

Gandesa, which would be where Walter would renew his quest come morning, so he drove off in that direction. For this entire day's labour he had discovered two worthwhile things. The most important one was that he was closing in on the place where Southcott had probably acquired his enduring memory. The other discovery was that motor-bikes were implements of the young.

Gandesa was a community nearer to what Walter believed Southcott might have been fascinated by. It was old, although it was also a moderately thriving community, and it was in a scenic setting that would make almost anyone stop and admire it.

It had two hostels, and at the first one Walter Whalen encountered his first stroke of genuine good luck. The wife of the proprietor had worked for four years as a domestic servant in England. She initially thought Walter Whalen was English and before he could explain she recalled, in her own inimitable English, the many places she had visited in Britain. By the time Walter got the idea across that as a matter of fact he was an American, not a Briton, the woman had just about exhausted her itinerary.

As an American, the woman viewed Walter Whalen as some very unique species of human being, like the English, but much richer and vastly more eccentric. She was perfectly willing to earn ten of Walter's American dollars, providing of course nothing indecent nor

146

illegal was involved.

What he wanted to know was whether, three years earlier, an American who had visited Gandesa, had met and talked to any particular people in the town. The woman arched magnificent eyebrows and raised her hands, palms up. Gandesa was not a village, it was a town; to procure this kind of information would be difficult. The woman might have to spend whole days asking around.

Inadvertently, she gave Walter Whalen his answer that Gandesa was not the place he sought. She asked if he would drive her around while she made enquiries, and when he turned to gaze out the wavy window at his motor-bike, with some uncomfortable thoughts beginning to form about this sort of thing, he saw nothing but paved roads.

Aphrodite in the *dust*...

He turned back, handed the woman ten American dollars, asked which room he might engage for the night, and said that he had changed his mind, that he would not require her services after all. She looked thoroughly baffled for a moment, then grandly raised her wide shoulders and let them fall with finality, and took him round to his room.

Obviously, all Americans were deranged.

CHAPTER SIXTEEN

A FEEL OF PAST AND PRESENT

Upon arriving in Villa Real Walter Whalen sought the hotel—which was an inn, actually, all on one floor and constructed of stone, with a low ceiling and a variety of conveniences better designated as *in*conveniences. Yet it had the kind of charm that went with ancient structures in quiet places. The room assigned to Walter had a window that looked out upon a small walled rear garden where someone, undoubtedly a woman, grew flowers and tended two olive trees whose trunks were as gnarled as age could make them. Birds quarrelled in the topmost branches, and the air was wine-scented, at least in the morning before the drenching Mediterranean sun rose high enough to be dominant.

The atmosphere of this village was different even from the atmosphere of Gandesa. It had nothing in common with a place like Tarragona or Barcelona, and for once Walter did not have that ostracised feeling: the sensation of being closed out because the people were so different and their language was incomprehensible to him. Some words he had picked up. It did not take long, in any foreign place, to learn, providing there was no

148

alternative.

Villa Real was partly plateaux, partly slope, but the tilted part, which was along the upper reaches of the village, had over the centuries been worn down until it no longer was at all steep. The lower, flatter part, had obviously been levelled off, the Lord only knew how long ago, by villagers. Below this flat part the terrain dropped off again in the direction of the lowlands, and continued to do so for some miles, so actually, Villa Real rested partly upon a man-made bench, and partly upon a very gentle uphill slope, but whether a person was in the upper section or the lower section, he had a splendid view towards the sea, in which direction the Ebro ran, and when dawnlight first appeared, it seemed to spill like molten gold from the rearward mountain heights towards the distant sea, bringing on a great change, whether it touched stone rooftops, trees, miles of tan-tawny dust, or the green richness of the distant coastlands.

Walter was not a man who was insensitive to natural beauty, to natural things, but over the years of his life he had not really been permitted the time to fully appreciate them, so when he stood out back of the inn making his first study of Villa Real, he was not as immediately impressed with the beauty as he was with the peculiar languor.

It was not just that the village was quiet at mid-morning, which was unusual in itself, but it was that the air of quiet had a definite feeling, not quite of languor and certainly not of laziness nor drowsiness, but of unshakeable serenity.

People, he saw, went about their work. Up the far mountainside a shepherd was taking his flock, and closer, south of the inn behind two houses, a pair of sturdy women were doing their laundry in a sort of arbour that Walter thought was shaded by grape vines growing up and over. There was a shop built onto the front of one of the ancient stone houses which fronted upon Villa Real's main thoroughfare—*only* thoroughfare in fact; elsewhere there were simply wide trails. Through the wide door of this shop a greying man with a lean, Moorish, face and a body of seasoned sinew and gristle, was working with leather.

Nearer, in fact only just across the wall of the inn's rear garden, a handsome woman, with a first dusting of grey at the temples, worked amid rows of vegetables. Her body was hard and coppery and as muscular as though she had done this kind of manual work all her life—which of course she had.

Yet despite the work, Villa Real was quiet, for the most part, and possessed of a feeling of antiquity, of fatalistic acceptance of that which was, and of that which was to be. Walter, who had never tasted goat's milk in his life, nor goat-milk cheese, sampled both at

150

mid-day, sharing with his host the innkeeper, a simple but adequate luncheon.

It was a little like attending a convention of mutes; gestures sufficed for the simplest things, but beyond that communication was next to impossible. Still, the Catalonian was a friendly man and probably, judging from the flash of his eye and the line of his wide mouth, he was also a fearless man, although that may have been more true thirty years back than it was now, when he seemed to be at least in his mid-fifties.

Later, Walter slow-paced the length of the village, and back again. He visited the church, which was surprisingly grand for the size of Villa Real, and out back, the church's cemetery. Here, pedantically overcoming his total lack of affinity for the language, he worked at making the proper pronunciations, at least making the proper *phonetic* pronunciations, which was a decent start. Here too, he read dates that went back a century prior to the discovery of the New World, and amid a pile of broken stones, evidently removed from more ancient graves, he found what looked like even more ancient grave markers.

The church—almost a cathedral in its massive grandness—was in the upper end of the village where the wide, dusty roadway began to definitely lift towards the backdrop mountains. The view from out front was

151

downhill. Walter could see the rooftops at the lowest end of the village, and he had an excellent sighting to his right and left, out back of the main roadway where the houses stood, almost indiscriminately spaced according to the uneven size of each garden plot that lay adjacent to the structures. If Villa Real had ever owned a grand residence, perhaps in the Middle Ages, there was no longer any trace of it, and yet it seemed that the town had, sometime in its past, been of some strategic value, for, aside from its access to the river, it was on both sides of a very ancient thoroughfare that came upwards from the coastlands, and passed through the centre of the village heading unerringly towards a distant wide break in the mountainous skyline.

Walter knew nothing of European history, but even in the New World towns that were situated as was Villa Real, had, in the past, served as first lines of defence from sea-going corsairs; they defended the hinterlands from blood-thirsty marauders who came by sail.

Well; whatever the past of Villa Real—and it was all around one to be felt and lived with—no man who drew breath into living tissue could do much more than wonder about it.

Walter went down through the shade on the far side of the roadway, back in the direction of the inn. He had his own peculiar problems, and they had nothing much in common with

152

the past; at least not with the very distant past.

Villa Real had no paved roadways. Standing out front of the inn partially concealed by shade and shadows, Walter looked steadily back up the way he had just come, towards the upper reaches of the village. Here, like this, would be how a tourist would have his first good look at Villa real. The sun was brilliant, up there, and much farther too, in fact, up where it made the mountainsides resemble burnished copper.

If a man were standing about in this spot, looking uphill at about, say, mid-day or even perhaps mid-afternoon, he would see anyone coming down the roadway *in the dust*, with all the uniqueness of Villa Real around them, and also with that magnificent Mediterranean sunlight soft-lying at their back.

Walter leaned upon the inn's rough front wall. He thought of the handsome woman out back in her vegetable rows, thought of her at, say, about twenty years of age with raven hair and magnificent shoulders and breasts and thighs, coming down towards the inn from the direction of, perhaps, the church, with a muscular stride.

My God, Aphrodite brought to earth in the dust of Spain.

The thought came as naturally as drawing a fresh breath. When he had wondered at this poetry in Charles Southcott, the hard-driving realist, he had done that wondering back in the

153

immaculate sterility of Boston General Hospital. Here, it was the most natural and easy thing in the world, to have such thoughts.

An old woman dressed in shapeless black came from a side-street on a meandering course, heading in the direction of the church. Walter watched her because there was no other motion. When she reached the worn, low and broad steps, she paused to adjust a head-covering, then she entered the church, and the roadway was empty again until several small, dark and very shiny chickens came from between two low stone buildings to explore the roadway dust, and sunshine.

Well; obviously neither the old woman nor the chickens qualified, but Walter was sure in his soul that this was the place Charles Southcott had remembered in his secret mind. Walter could almost visualise the exquisite woman coming towards him from the upper end of the village, and she would be a gut-wrenching handsome, probably even more handsome, as the woman out back in her vegetable patch had been.

Villa Real *did* have beautiful women in it. He had seen people passing the inn, going in one direction or the other, and although their impression upon him had been negligible until now, he had recognised the perfection because he was more a man than a biologist.

He had also seen a priest—whose gown seemed indelibly stained at ground-level—and he had seen several shepherds, and any number of the dark men with their hawkish, Moorish, profiles.

It would have helped immeasurably if there had been someone, like the woman over at Gandesa, who spoke English, because it seemed clear that to appreciate a place as alien as this, Walter Whalen needed to know about the background, the past, the customs and the convictions, of Villa Real's people.

He strolled southward then westward through the back byways, saw children as fair in their skin-tones but as dark-eyed as gypsies, laughing at their play like children everywhere. He saw grave old men whose colouring was at times darker even than the land, and he saw brisk housewives, sturdy and doe-eyed, some young, mostly older, in their gardens, and going back and forth from goat-sheds to residences.

The nearer it got to evening the more the fragrances changed, and in the utterly still air, it was possible to catch the scent of cooking.

In Villa Real life seemed to be lived one day at a time. From morning until evening people did whatever was essential to the business of immediate existence, and small comfort. The noticeable lack of frenzy made its impression upon Walter. Here, he could hardly conceive of a single man arising before five in the morning in order to reach an operating room before seven o'clock, nor afterwards, spending

155

a full day which might last as long as fifteen or sixteen hours, at his profession. On the other hand he had no difficulty believing that, under the proper stimulus, these foreign people would accomplish momentous things, but far less for personal gain than for some ideological reason that might completely destroy them. And they would do those things on an empty stomach.

As the shadows began coming in soft layers inland and uphill from the distant sea, Walter turned slowly to pace back in the direction of the inn.

A dog came to stand stiff-legged and stare as Walter passed. It neither barked nor offered to slip in from behind and bite. Some she-goats with the fierce-foolish expression of their kind, came boldly to the edge of stone-piled pen fences and stared too, but with nothing more ominous to them than frank curiosity.

A lean Spaniard passed with a grave glance and a kindly nod. Walter returned the nod but suppressed the smile he usually used with it, and wondered why these people were so sparing with smiles. He decided it was the natural reserve of mountain-dwellers, and remembered that during his boyhood in West Virginia, there had been a similar dignified reserve. Here, it would be more understandable; he was a foreigner. No doubt, Villa Real being no larger than it was, by now word had spread that he was here. The innkeeper had been interested in him, and undoubtedly that sturdy, volatile individual could be counted upon to enhance his community standing by dispensing information. Walter smiled, West Virginia was like *that*, too, except that the prime disseminator of information and gossip had been the proprietor of the general store.

He turned up the road towards the inn and unconsciously lifted his glance to the uphill stretch of roadway. But, although there were people abroad, Aphrodite was not among them.

Farther back, discernible only by the lazy-rising tan dust that hung in the dull red of ending day, a flock of sheep and goats were coming down the mountainside, homeward bound, no doubt, from their daylong foraging.

Walter paused at the doorway of the inn to speculate that this same scene had probably existed in the vicinity of Villa Real for a thousand years. Perhaps for two thousand years. Then he ducked his head at the door-lintel and went inside, his first day in the village drawing to a close.

CHAPTER SEVENTEEN

ONE WHO SPEAKS ENGLISH

Nothing could happen in Villa Real without the priest knowing of it, neither the birth of a child nor the arrival of a foreigner, and although the first of these events was the re-enactment of a miracle, it happened often enough to preclude it from being the great event that the arrival of a stranger inevitably was.

Villa Real was not on a tourist byway, nor was there really anything in the village that could normally be expected to entice tourists, at least those from far lands, to remain in the village for any extended period of time.

People came each spring and autumn from Madrid, and from France, but they seldom lingered longer than was required to stroll the length of Villa Real, and perhaps take a few pictures. The village was undeniably picturesque; but throughout Europe, if a person chose to seek them out, there were other villages just as old and just as picturesque, and just as serenely dull.

As Father Ordoñez said to Pablo Holquin, the innkeeper, if the newcomer had settled in for a week, and if he had no knowledge of either the language or the countryside, then whatever his purpose in being in Villa Real had to be, it was not, in all probability, the same reason that attracted most tourists who arrived each spring and autumn in the morning and who departed in the afternoon.

'And if he is as you think, a German, Pablo, then all this is even more unusual. Between us there is a memory of those ones.'

'Yes, Father,' conceded the innkeeper, 'but of that I am not certain. He could be an Englishman.'

Father Ordoñez was a wiry aesthete with a narrow face and dark grey eyes. He looked to be—and he was—a man of strong orthodox views. In another time he would have been the one to apply the torch to the faggot-pyre of an heretic, and yet in his youth, as in the youth of the innkeeper, he had shed blood in a cause as alien to Christian doctrine as any cause ever devised. Like Pablo Holquin, Francisco Ordoñez, had been an unswerving supporter of the *Falange*, of the Order of Fasces. Perhaps it was not at all odd that this narrow-faced man preached godliness and still believed in the *Falange*, because while it was entirely possible for a man to venerate humility, it was equally possible for him to be genetically incapable of being humble, even though he believed that he was. Not odd at all, for as a matter of fact there were far more unconscious hypocrites in the world than there were conscious ones.

As for the tourist being an Englishman,

159

Father Ordoñez who sympathised with the Generalissimo's claim to Gibraltar, considered this possibility as being even more distasteful; at least Germans made a lot of noise when they came, while the English, well, of the English it was universally known that they were a subtle and devious lot.

Still, there was nothing at Villa Real. No untouched treasure, no particularly desirable trade. So, whether the stranger was German or English, what could possibly be his purpose in the village.

'He takes pictures, Pablo?'

'No, Father. He arrived without a camera. Just a German motorcycle.'

'Ah ha, then he *is* a German.'

The innkeeper hunched his thick shoulders, and loosened them. 'Who knows? Of this I can tell you of a certainty: he does not respond to German. I remember a few words. I purposefully tried them on him. But it may be, as I have heard, that the Germans are as ignorant of distant dialects as we are.'

'Did you try any English words?'

'Father, I know none to try. That is why I came to see you. If there is another person in Villa Real who speaks English, I have never discovered him.'

Father Ordoñez was keen on the scent. 'Yes, of a certainty, Pablo, and you have done precisely right. Now, is this stranger at the inn?'

'Yes, Father. He is getting ready for dinner. I
160

slipped out the side door and came hastily to you. It is in my mind that you could conceivably happen to stop through this evening, and I could then perform the introduction, and if this man does indeed subscribe to English, why then, Father, you could interrogate him. No?'

Father Ordoñez did not smile, but he was probably pleased. 'Very well. Now you go back, and in due time I shall happen through.'

The innkeeper had no difficulty arriving back at his establishment, and the handsome woman with a dusting of first grey at her temples, who was his wife, already had a meal half-prepared with vegetables from the soil beyond the garden wall, for whatever kind of man their guest was, he was a man, and men liked good food.

The woman did not ask where her man had been. She had the kind of faith in him habit and resignation engendered. He had not been drinking, obviously, or she would have smelled that, and he had not been gone long to have been gambling, and, as for that other thing, she had never worried, for she was as much woman as he ever was a man. So—'Take the plate to the table of our stranger, and remember—if he is a German he will want to taste the wine and if he is an Englishman, he will probably want to smell it, then taste it.' She raised liquid dark eyes. 'Or is it the other way around?'

Walter did neither. He simply poured a little,

a very sparing little, of the red wine into his glass, and for most of the meal it sat there untouched. Americans, except for those raised in immigrant ghettoes, were not notably wine-drinkers. What Walter Whalen would have much preferred was a double scotch-and-soda, but of course that was out. He did not even try to explain; he had no idea what hand-gestures served to get across either the idea of scotch, or of soda.

The meal was filling. It was no epicurean's source of ecstasy, but he could easily imagine someone climbing mountains on this kind of diet. He was leary of the meat. It was spiced beyond any simple recognition, for which he was warily thankful because, remembering those staring goats throughout the village, he had some idea that what he was eating was only very distantly related to beef, which under normal circumstances was the mainstay of his diet.

Finally, he drank the wine. It took, had the kind of muscle that would sustain a man up a mountainside, but it would never do well in Massachusetts. Of course it would never have to make the effort.

As he sat, the solitary diner in the black-beamed, low-ceilinged dining-room, dwelling gloomily upon something that was probably causing a furore three or four thousand miles away, in Boston—his disappearance—a lean, sallow-faced man cast a thin shadow forward

162

from the roadside entrance. Walter looked up. The newcomer was a priest. Walter recognised the man; he had caught a number of sightings of this thin figure, and even from a distance the impression had come strongly, and not quite favourably. Now, the priest nodded, so Walter returned the nod, and as the priest came forward Walter had the same feeling over again but much stronger as the priest got closer.

In accented English the priest said, 'Good evening. I suppose a man unable to speak our language must feel lonely in Villa Real.'

All of Walter's wary antipathies vanished. It was like being offered a tall glass of cold water on a blazing-hot day to hear someone speak comprehensibly. He offered the priest a chair, and although the priest smiled, such was the narrow, predatory configuration of his face that it was difficult to believe in the sincerity of that smile.

There was an extra glass so Walter offered wine. The priest accepted, and as Walter poured, he felt the dark grey eyes probing. It made his wariness return. Nor was it hard to imagine what this lean, lipless devout wanted: to know who Walter was and why he was lingering in Villa Real.

Well; there was nothing unusual about this particular attitude in small towns, whether in Spain or America. Strangers were natural sources of speculation and curiosity. *Foreign* strangers even more so.

He finished filling the glass and set the bottle aside, and as the priest lifted the glass Walter reached a decision that he had considered since first arriving in France. He had done nothing about it there, for the elemental reason that he had not been required to; no one had been interested in his name or his point of origin. Here, in Spain, no one had been interested—up until now—either. But now they would be, and he had the time to fabricate a lie. He could manage it without difficulty because he had already half-arrived at the point where he felt the lie was necessary.

At least it would not hurt anyone.

The priest said, 'You are English, perhaps, my friend?'

Walter was tempted, but at the last moment he foresaw the complications and opted for the truth. 'American, Father. Herbert Smith, from Omaha, Nebraska, U.S.A.'

The priest had one of those habitually closed faces. It showed nothing as he repeated this. 'Herbert Smith from the United States of America.'

The innkeeper arrived and briefly hovered, then withdrew. Walter gazed after the man, beginning to quietly wonder. Not that it mattered, but this priest was hardly the type to be an official greeter—if there were such a thing in Villa Real.

'And you are a tourist,' said the priest, trying

164

to raise his weak smile again.

Walter smiled back. 'A tourist, Father. I have been in France, and having never been to Spain, decided to make the trip.' Walter leaned back, still smiling. 'Villa Real is something—well—poignantly picturesque, to me.' Walter held the priest's attention without effort. 'Three years ago a friend of mine came through here. A man named Southcott, Charles Southcott. He was very impressed. That was three years ago, Father.'

As though uncomfortably, or perhaps vaguely, aware that the lapse of time was important, Father Ordoñez said, 'Three years ago.' Then he lifted, and dropped, thin, narrow shoulders. 'I would not remember, I think.'

'A large, thick, fair-complexioned man, Father. He was driven here by a man from Reus who owns a car and hires himself out with it to drive tourists through the countryside.'

The priest was polite. 'Yes, of course. This man with the car may drive a number of people each season. Three years is a long time, no? And this friend of yours—I'm sure I didn't meet him, did I?'

Walter almost despaired, but not quite. 'I don't recall him mentioning you, Father. He spent most of one day here. The car-owner told me that.'

'Yes. Well; it is possible, of course.' Father Ordoñez pushed past this preoccupation with

165

the other American, the one who came and saw, and departed, three years earlier. 'Do you find Villa Real as your friend said it was, then?' Walter nodded, his hopes dwindling. Obviously, this man did not recall Charles Southcott, and probably there was no reason why he should; Southcott was hardly the type to go looking for a village priest. And yet this was a disappointment. In its wake came another thought: the priest now knew what Walter wanted—to find someone who remembered seeing his friend named Southcott. He hesitated about making his standard offer of ten dollars for information, though. After a moment of casting about he said, 'Well, Father, I was very impressed by the things my friend told me. If there were someone he talked to, I would like to meet them so perhaps I could see the same things.'

Father Ordoñez's grey eyes showed a trace of puzzlement, but he said nothing to indicate that he was troubled. Instead, he agreed to ask round, and if he found anyone Charles Southcott could have met, he would let Walter know. Otherwise, he said, he would be delighted to take Walter round and show him what there was to see.

Walter showed gratitude and promised to look Father Ordoñez up, eventually. At the end of this topic, the priest finished his wine and departed, and when the innkeeper returned Walter smiled and the man smiled

166

back, a little guiltily, Walter thought, which answered the question about Father Ordoñez's casual arrival while Walter was at dinner.

Later, outside in the pleasant night, Walter had a stray thought: if the innkeeper, and now the parish priest, passed along the gossip about the American staying at the inn, and of course providing Southcott's misplaced psyche was indeed in this place, and providing, too, that it were capable of remembering, then perhaps Walter would not have to look for *it*, perhaps *it* might come looking for him.

He stood utterly still for a long time considering this prospect. If Southcott's psyche *did* possess the missing segments of the man's memory bank, then it would recall very well where it had been before arriving here in Villa Real, perhaps in the mind and body of some beautiful girl—Southcott's Aphrodite in the dust—and granting the possibility of this, then Walter might be in some kind of peril.

It could be one thing for Southcott to recall his Spanish Aphrodite, and something totally different for him to discover that *he had become her*.

CHAPTER EIGHTEEN

NEWS FROM HOME

When Pablo Holquin made his semi-monthly trip to Tarragona he normally had his wife along. She was exceptionally capable at bartering. He was, too, but she was better at it, except that when he went down to the coast this time, he had to leave her behind because of the paying guest. One could hardly take a person's money for room and board, and then not board them.

Well; Pablo Holquin was a long way from being a child. If the merchants of Tarragona were astute, so was the villager from Villa Real.

Walter did not miss the innkeeper. He had been at Villa Real almost a full week now, and had begun to make some distinctions. For example, he knew that the handsome woman he had seen out back in the vegetable garden, was his host's wife. He had also observed that Father Ordoñez was a zealot about bringing his recalcitrants to the church, and that the man with the leather-working shop on the front of his house drank wine in slow swallows all day long, without managing to be drunk.

He had wrung a smile from some of the villagers, while from others he got a mixed look, as though they were not quite sure

168

whether an American was someone to like or to avoid. There was an old scandal about an American aircraft accidentally dropping some bombs upon a Spanish beach, and someone had said Americans based at an airfield down in Málaga were constantly causing trouble in the towns and villages.

What he had *not* done was devise a method for determining which of the beautiful women of Villa Real might have been Charles Southcott's Spanish Aphrodite, and that was uppermost in his mind, although he had not considered his course if she turned up. But that troubled him a lot less than it might have; so far, in this bizarre business, he had taken one step at a time, and so far that had proved satisfactory.

At dinner the evening he first ventured into the uphill countryside, with an appetite like a horse, the innkeeper made a flourish and presented Walter with a newspaper—in English. This was the first inkling Whalen had that his host had been to the seacoast for supplies. He accepted the newspaper—which was actually published in Madrid—with genuine gratitude, not doubting for one moment but that its price would be added to his bill, yet pleased to get it nonetheless.

Until he read the second page. The front page had nothing but Continental news. The second page had a sensational story of a great scandal in America, written, obviously, by someone whose command of English was excellent, but who was definitely not an American, because in the reporting of this exposé, there was an undercurrent of vindictive delight, as though the reporter could not restrain his great pleasure over a calamity in the U.S.A. It was not, actually, a fresh approach to America—reporting at all, but Walter did not know this. After he had read half through the revelation, he was gripped by the salient factors and by them alone.

In Boston, Massachusetts, it had come to light within the past few days that a member of a prominent Boston hospital had, through diabolical and illegal experimentation, caused the intellectual deterioration of one of America's most prominent capitalists, Charles Southcott. The police were currently making a rigorous search for this physician, Doctor Walter Whalen, a man eminent in the fields of hypertension and circulatory disabilities, who had completely disappeared.

A legal action for damages in excess of five million dollars had been filed by the wife of the ailing entrepreneur, Charles Southcott, naming Doctor Whalen, Boston General Hospital, and the State of Massachusetts, as well as the City of Boston.

In what the newspaper writer termed a 'hideously grisly experiment upon a completely helpless hospital patient,' it was stated that Doctor Whalen, like the creator of

170

the mythical monster Frankenstein, only worse because Whalen used a living human being for *his* heinous experiment, had created a living, functioning, mindless vegetable, out of a man known worldwide, and respected, for his previous great astuteness and business acumen.

The chief of Boston General Hospital and several members of his staff had been removed from their positions, although it was stated that Doctor Whalen had performed his terrible crime without their knowledge, pending a thorough investigation of the bizarre circumstances surrounding this unprecedented disaster in American medical history.

Walter put the paper aside. There were several more columns but he had read enough. The world had fallen upon John Ames and Boston General. If the story rated the second page of this English-language foreign paper, Walter could imagine how the press at home was handling it. There would even be pictures of him, and probably some garbled science-fiction attempt to explain how his innovation had been supposed to work.

It did not occur to him right then, but it did later, that fortunately the newspaper Mister Holquin—*Señor* Holquin—had brought back, had no photograph of the infamous American doctor.

He did not finish his dinner, but when he went out for a stroll in the bland night, he had the newspaper tucked into a pocket.

He had known this would happen, inevitably; had known when he had decided to come to Spain that he was running as much as he was seeking an answer to the riddle that obsessed him.

The shock should not have been this bad, perhaps, but it was; in fact it was worse. It forced him to face his current predicament, and that almost brought him to panic. He had never been in serious trouble before in his life, and like all responsible people who believed in law and order, he had a positive conviction that the law could find anyone it set out to find. Even Herbert Smith from Omaha, Nebraska, U.S.A.

He walked from one end of Villa Real to the other without being aware of his surroundings until, far downhill on the roadway leading to the coastlands, he had to pause to rest, because he had been almost running.

There was no moon and the sea-winds that swept inland most evenings and nights to keep the air clean and fresh, were little more than a sigh tonight. There were stars across a flawless firmament, and where the rearward mountains slanted heavenward in patternless disarray, the night was as black as ink.

Walter sat upon a smooth mile-marker at the roadside visualising John Ames with his back to the wall, visualising Littleton and Swansinger, and all the others. He could almost hear their bitterness, their angry recriminations, and through it all Charles Southcott lay as inert as ever with no reason to hope he would ever lie—or feel—differently.

For him, thankfully, there would be no crisis, and no turmoil nor tragedy. He was helpless. He was also placidly without hope. For his wife it would be a much different matter, and for everyone else it would be different too.

Ironically, the person who had been injured was unable to comprehend the tragedy, but those who would, eventually, after a sufficient passage of time—maybe years and years— resume the threads of their lives, had it at least in their favour that they *could* recover. The only two people on earth who were really and deeply involved, Charles Southcott, the vegetable, and Walter Whalen, the infamous experimenter, would never recover unless Walter Whalen were able to, in some manner he had no idea about at all, locate the misplaced Southcott-psyche and devise a way to get it back where it belonged.

How?

He did not attempt an answer to that. He did not even want to speculate about it. He had to doggedly persevere in what he was currently doing, and if—*if*—this were successful, *then* he would take the next step.

His mood quieted a little at a time, but the new sensation, added to the old hauntings—

173

being a fugitive from the law—brought on a grim doggedness that made him more than ever resolved.

If he succeeded in making Charles Southcott whole again—what then? There still would not be a hospital that would have him, and if he re-built a private practice elsewhere—assuming the American Medical Association would permit it—without much doubt this thing was going to follow him. He could imagine the appelations that would accrue: The Mad Scientist, the Practitioner of the Dark Arts, *et cetera.*

Arising from the mile-marker and looking back up towards Villa Real, he saw himself as the *real* victim; Charles Southcott, back at Boston General, not only had no knowledge whatsoever of what had happened to him, but he also had a vast fortune which would take care of him in comfort and security for as long as he lived. The others, Ames and Boston General, would eventually achieve vindication. Only Walter Whalen was the *real* victim; for him there would never again be peace of mind. As he began strolling up towards the village he reflected upon the bitter irony of a man who sought to bring something good to mankind, being destroyed by his own humanitarianism.

When he got back to the inn the place was dark. The entire village was dark, except for an ectoplasmic-type nightglow compounded of moonlight and starshine, which reflected most notably off the domed peak of the church, and which also reflected off the tile and flag roofs of residences and stores. If Walter had been in the mood, he could have seen how Villa Real really looked, now, exactly as it had looked three, four, five hundred years ago. Instead, he went silently to his room at the back of the inn, got ready for bed, and now that the shock had passed, more or less, he gazed out the window with a calm detachment, wondering what recourse a fugitive from the law had?

He was probably as safe right where he was, as he would be anywhere. Newspapers in Villa Real were certainly not especially rare, but neither were they commonplace, and even the ones that did show up, were unlikely to carry photographs of a notorious American physician as long as more critical matters touching upon conditions in Europe would be of more interest to Europeans, particularly, to Spaniards.

Moreover, if he fled again, this time he would have to abandon his purpose for being at Villa Real. He would have to become nothing more nor less than a common fugitive, and that had absolutely no appeal at all. Perhaps, in time, he might begin to think as a fugitive, but right now he was still thinking in terms of The Riddle.

By the time he climbed into bed to lie back listening to the tiny night-sounds from beyond the window, out in the garden, he was back once more trying to devise some method for locating Charles Southcott's Aphrodite. He was that calm.

Sleep came in mid-thought, and with it the dissolution of Self and the scattering of all the separate parts until morning when everything was slowly gathered together again, as Walter Whalen awakened—to the sound of a rooster fight somewhere just beyond the garden wall, outside.

He lay relaxed for a long while, watching how the fresh softness of newlight firmed up along the far wall of his room, and because the plastering had been done by hand, either none too skilled, or perhaps applying the coating over an uneven under-layer of mortared stone, he saw the lower places brighten last. In America the walls did not have low places, they were meticulously perfect. Nor did bedrooms in America have low ceilings with ancient hand-squared beams; in America ceilings were sweeping and soaring and crushingly impersonal. There was a rough adze mark upon a rafter near the middle of Walter's room, where a powerful blow delivered by a strong arm had cut a little too deeply. It was someone's distinctive mark; he had been gone probably several hundred years. Probably no one now even remembered his name, yet there was his mark, and from it, Walter could conjure a whole man; dark and industrious and

176

physically powerful. American ceilings and walls were like the impersonal walls of a mausoleum; the people who created them came and went without a sound, and no one wanted them to leave a flaw behind.

Walter heaved up out of bed wondering if Charles Southcott hadn't caught some kind of momentary illumination about life, while he had been here in Villa Real three years ago, and it was this, perhaps as much as his Aphrodite in the dust that made the memory so strong ever afterwards.

Walter was able, by now, to *feel* the village, not to just see it. He even wondered if perhaps he and Charles Southcott's psyche were not actually voluntary exiles *from* something, not especially *to* it. If they were not actually seeking something in order to escape from something worse.

CHAPTER NINETEEN

AN OLD MEANING RENEWED

The clouds that cast shadows earthward as soon as they reached land from out over the Mediterranean, were harbinger's of the invisible wind. If they rode swiftly, then there was a high wind at their backs. If they came gently from the sea towards the mountains, then there would be no wind down lower where Iberia lay, like the seamed and mottled palm of a fingerless hand.

Slow clouds meant winey days, and such was the marvel of a woman in conception that warmth and fragrance and beauty went deeper than the skin, went cleanly to the sensing soul bringing on a sensation of wonder and of sweet softness. A woman with child did not *have* a secret, she *was* a secret.

There was nothing unusual about Maria's feelings. She leaned in the bronzed shade by the stone pen watching as the flock trudged dutifully towards the foothill pasturage, and felt herself to be part of the slow-drifting high clouds, felt herself drawing new life from the old sun, and felt herself as much of the mountainslope and the clear air, as of the soil and the village.

It was as though she had finally ceased to skim upon the surface of life, the *true* miracle, and had become at one with everything she could see or feel or know.

Juan had laughed softly at her when she had tried to explain. He was a gentle man, and yet lately there seemed to be a little assertion, a little more definitiveness of thought and purpose and action. She had only noticed it that night several weeks earlier when he had loved her under the full moon and among the olive trees.

He had laughed and had kissed her, and had

said he would bring the flock back early this afternoon, because he'd had an idea she might be lonely. He had left with a wicked look, so she understood exactly what he meant about her being lonely. Men!

She raised both arms to the tree at her side and considered the sun through dusty leaves. God was good. As Juan had said, there has to be a reason, and there most certainly is a purpose; the fact that God alone knows both changed nothing; in His own good time he does what must obtain, and it was a good sign that now, finally, she was with Juan's child, for as her husband had said, if people persisted in striving hard to go against the will of God, why then, unhappy results followed. But *they* had *not* gone against His will; they had been very patient, so now that He had nodded and Maria had conceived, well then, without question this child of theirs would be a most beautiful and delightful one.

She turned at the faint sound of leather over stone and saw Father Ordoñez approaching, his narrow face grave and his thin body leaning to the slight incline. When he saw her watching he called a little greeting, to which she responded as she left the tree and went round to the front of the stone pen to meet him about half-way.

Father Ordoñez had already seen the distant dust; what vexed him was that he had been unable to see it until he got this far towards the upper end of the village. If he had seen it earlier he would not have bothered to make this walk. What he had come about was not important anyway. Well; not all *that* important. He could easily have waited until he saw either Maria or Juan down nearer his stone cottage out back of the church. Or even in church, for that matter, because they never missed a Sunday. Not since Father Ordoñez had married them, had they missed a service.

He paused in the sunlight, saw without understanding why, that Maria's face was softer and rounder and more beautiful, and that her expression was sweetly radiant. Well; he had known for several years that there was no woman in Villa Real whose beauty could compare, and so much for that. Father Ordoñez's asceticism had long ago dried up any masculine juices; even before he had become of the church, the generic austerity of his Spartan character had begun to do that.

He said, 'Juan goes earlier to the pasturage these days,' and averted his narrow face to study the distant dust.

Maria was complacent about this, as about many other things. 'He told me that this is the best way, for a man who will have the care of a family, Father.'

The priest brought his thin face around quickly. 'Yes. Well then, I understand, and I am happy for you both.'

Maria smiled and did not look away.

Another time she might have been confused or embarrassed. Not now, not with the priest who had gone to such lengths to explain how the mysterious workings of God's will achieved harmony in the fullness of time, and that people simply had to be patient, standing there with her, sharing the marvel of her secret.

'He will return early, though,' she explained, wanting to linger longer over the other thing, but knowing how men were, choosing instead to get back to whatever the point of this visit was. 'By mid-afternoon, he said.'

Father Ordoñez accepted this, but he had still made the hike up here, so he said, 'You have heard of the American staying at Holquin's inn, no doubt.'

Maria had heard, but she had hardly heeded this scrap of gossip. Not now, although several weeks earlier she would have heeded it. Now, there was no room for even anything as unique as a tourist who came, and who stayed. She had not mentioned this to Juan; their lives had changed completely, lately. Nothing existed but each other, and their miracle.

'I have heard, yes,' she replied.

'He is interested in our countryside, Maria, and it came to me that Juan, who knows the mountains better than any of the other young men, could show him things. Well; like that old Roman ruin, the stone watchtower up there on the mountainside. He could let the American see how those ancient people started the stone

181

viaduct up where that spring is. And from the heights, he could show this man the whole country, and he could do it all without taking time off from the herding.'

Maria thought this could be arranged. 'I'll tell him,' she said, 'and he can come down and talk with you.'

Father Ordoñez was satisfied. He was also thirsty, so they went together to the stone house where he got water, then he departed and went back down the incline in the direction of his church, and the flatter part of Villa Real.

Maria had housework to do, and after that there was the laundry to be cared for, things that normally were little epics of drudgery but which became, now, responsibilities of a woman whose world was expanding a day at a time towards the full realisation of her oneness with all Creation.

Also, she had intended to go up the mountainside, later, the way she had been doing, without any real pattern to it, for several years, because within another few months it would probably be a hard climb, too hard for a woman swollen with child.

Only today she would not have to go the full distance. She worked, and stepped to the door now and then to glance at the moving sun. Her idea was to start up as Juan was starting down. They would meet and she would not have to go the full distance.

Out front Emilio Sanchez shuffled past,

bound for the distant places he went, for what purpose only he really knew, for although he usually came back with faggots or building stones, he had not owned a flock in many years, and that had been, long ago, the reason he went to the slopes.

Perhaps now it was simply habit with the old man. Or he might know of a place where a man with a sadness behind his smile could be alone. Whatever it was, Maria instinctively knew that for Emilio Sanchez this was his Reason, exactly as Maria's Reason was the bringing of life, not the melancholy recollection of its loss.

The sun moved with its inexorable serenity from right to left, and when the time was right Maria left the house for the stony trail. Up ahead, small against the dished-lift of the cardboard-coloured hillside, the old one moved with the certainty of a man and the haste of an ant.

Maria's stride was paced to the distance and to the climb. Since she could remember she had gone up to the hills, and in fact her initial lesson in discipline had come here. She had impatiently hurried, at first, and had been forced to sit and rest so that if she had been pacing herself, she would still have made as good time at the climbing. It took a little while to appreciate that the mountain did not care whether she panted with exasperation or whether she arrived on the slopes rested and fresh.

There was a wide place where a spring, long-since dried up, had made a little level landing. Here, she usually stopped to look backwards and downwards out over the village as far as the coast-mists, if they were present, allowed one to see. Farther, if the day was bell-clear. As much as a hundred and more miles towards the dark green of the rich lowlands.

Today, when she stopped and turned, breathing deeply, she saw a hiker towards the west, in which direction lay the town of Montblanch. He walked a bit, and rested, and if he had any purpose it was hard to imagine what it could be since the man did not appear to be following a trail.

He did not appear to understand that accosting high slopes was a matter of personal ability, either. Or perhaps it was simply that he had not the lungs for this kind of thing.

She wondered without any real interest who he might be, and as she turned to press onward it occurred to her that this might be the American. It probably was, since anyone from the village would not have hiked like that, and the American, as far as she had heard, was the only tourist in Villa Real.

All this freshened in her mind Father Ordoñez's purpose in paying his call earlier in the day. She probably would have remembered anyway, but now she most certainly would.

There was dust in the upper distance, thin, as always, and dun coloured. Juan was coming down. Of old Emilio there was not a sign, but then he could have veered right or left, the hills were full of long ridges and fissures. Erosion had carved them over the millenias, was still carving them but not as strongly as it once had because now there were protruding rocks of enormous size and weight to turn aside the chocolate freshets caused by heavy rainfall.

She stopped beside a hoary stone block, quarried by no-one-knew, but definitely squared with mathematical precision—perhaps by the Romans; their artifacts cropped up all the time—and sat down with the sunlight reaching deep within the murky folds and arroyos to bring heat and light to the things growing in those gloomy places, watching the flock as it streamed homeward. Of her husband there was no sight, but then there would not be anyway, as yet, because, even if the dust hadn't obscured him the distance might have; shepherds walked at the extreme end of their moving bands.

She leaned back, arms behind her, stiffened to support her upper body, and felt sunheat upon the firm thrust of both breasts, felt warmth upon her lower legs, and closed her eyes for a moment of quiet thoughtlessness.

Juan had teased her; a woman and a cow both bore their young nine months. At her resentment of this comparison he had laughed.

Ever since she could remember, Juan Valdez had possessed the most beautiful smile she had ever seen a man wear. But he had never laughed aloud very much. Although now he did. Always before, when they had been much younger, Juan had hung in an agony of self-consciousness when they had been alone together; even after they had been married he had remained diffident and embarrassed about some things. Not now.

So this, then, was how a man changed after giving away part of himself in order to make a woman also change.

Maria opened her eyes, seeking the distant figure. When she saw him her heart barely struck, then went on again as powerfully as before.

There was so much to be learned; so much that no one had ever tried to explain. She held no resentment at all. In fact making all these discoveries was like picking up the little precious leaves of autumn one at a time; when a person's hand was full, they had a treasure.

She heard the lead-goat bleat once or twice, then she could hear the rest of it, the rattle of little stones, the click of cloven feet, the garrulous whimpering of the eternally dissatisfied sheep, and the soft, fluting call of Juan when he saw her down there sitting on the Roman block.

The sun was half off its middle apex by this time. Before she and Juan got the flock penned for the night it would be two-thirds of the way on down, which was about as it had been that

186

special night between the stone pen and the olive trees, out back.

Tonight, of course, they would go there again. For whatever possible reason had her husband wanted to bring the flock down early? She smiled, knowing very well why.

She arose from the block as the animals started streaming past. Oh yes; there was the message from Father Ordoñez. She'd almost forgot, after all.

CHAPTER TWENTY

A TOUCH OF HANDS

For seven days Juan Valdez had followed the flock to the mountains and while it browsed he had sat motionless feeling within himself the gradually diminishing tumult.

The weaker will had not quite succumbed and the stronger will had not quite triumphed. It took those seven days for the melding to quieten, and what Charles Southcott remembered was no longer vivid and what Juan Valdez knew was no longer uppermost.

It seemed that in time Charles Southcott would no longer temporise; that what was environmentally real and of solid substance, would like the view as he sat clasping his knees looking far outward and downward, and the warm sun on his shoulders, provide the catalyst. As would the warm, golden arms of Maria, and this life he lived that filled his soul with a quiet and rich satisfaction.

But for the first few days he had lived a silent nightmare alleviated only by the needs and the hungers of both men, and these had been assuaged by Maria Peralta Valdez until now, after his second night of purest magic among the olive trees with his wife, she and the serenity of his existence, with her at the centre of it, mattered most above all things.

No more Margaret, no more bruising himself in the headlong rush to forget the restless unhappiness by accumulating wealth, and most promising of all, this melding of the stronger will with the weaker one until, as he could feel within himself, eventually there would be a new Juan Valdez and no Charles Southcott at all.

And that, he told himself after the seventh day, was precisely what he wanted most of all from life.

Then, when they were lying drowsily side by side in the wane of a crooked moon, she had told him of Father Ordoñez's visit and its purpose. She had said it as though ridding herself of an obligation, but somehow he knew that beyond the soft-sighing drowsiness of her words there was a fresh fear to be considered.

All the next day upon the slope he thought of that man at Holquin's inn.

He was almost certain who that American would turn out to be. If only the stranger had not arrived for another few months, until Charles Southcott was completely sublimated in Juan Valdez ... but the American had not waited, and Charles Southcott still had sufficient recall to remember. He knew for a fact he had never been in greater peril than he was at this moment. How the American would be able to change things back—to Margaret, to that mausoleum of a cold and stifling household, to the claw and fang world of finance and subterfuge and big business, he had no idea. But he *did* realise that if this stranger in the village was indeed Walter Whalen, he was the only living person who knew what had happened to Charles Southcott. Otherwise Doctor Whalen would not be down there at the inn. If Doctor Whalen had traced Charles Southcott—the Lord knew how—to Villa Real, then he might even already know how to make the change-back.

Logic warned him that the Charles Southcott psyche was not as yet thoroughly enough embedded in the ethos of Juan Valdez to be permanent, but even if it were, since Whalen had peeled it off, or out, once before, he might be able to do it again.

The fatalism of Juan Valdez would never have countenanced what the forceful will of predatory Charles Southcott thought next, but even if it had, the passivity of Juan Valdez

189

would have frozen him at the thought of carrying it through.

If that were indeed Doctor Whalen down there, the only man alive who could possibly know what had happened to the misplaced Southcott psyche, he was the only threat to the steadily emerging new Juan Valdez, and to ensure that this slow melding were not interfered with, Doctor Whalen would have to be forever kept silent.

Juan arose as usual when the shadows were of a correct spacing and length, called up his flock and headed it for the lowlands.

Charles Southcott could not, of course, have a second chance because, obviously, life did not function according to any such law. But Juan Valdez had not begun to spend himself, so his chance still lay ahead. In short words, Juan Valdez at twenty-four years of age, had a lifetime ahead of him, and Charles Southcott at forty-four had already lived more than half *his* lifetime. An additional twenty years of life, plus the possession of a woman of warm and hungering fullness, plus a serenity of soul and spirit unknown to Charles Southcott, were all the reason a man needed, to do, somehow, what had to be done, and if he did it as Charles Southcott, by the time Southcott was lost in the new soul of Juan Valdez, he could not possibly remember ever having done it.

The trail down was familiar stone by stone, as were the friendly shadows, as were the mute-blind hips and round flanks of the mountainslopes, as well as the rooftops and meandering roadways of his village growing softer with the passing of the red-copper Mediterranean sun. The sooner Charles Southcott were sublimated and only gentle Juan Valdez remained, the better.

The lead-goat played pranks the last hundred yards and Maria waved a cloth from out back by the stone pen where she waited. He lifted an arm, then dropped it and strode ahead with an ache under his heart for what had to be done in order to preserve this life which he valued and which he wanted above all other lives.

Later, as they stood, as usual, watching the flock crowd to water, he felt her close enough to rub him at hip and shoulder. He leaned down to brush her throat with his lips and she raced to the house leaving him to look, and smile.

Later, with dusk down all around, he trudged down to the centre of Villa real to find Father Ordoñez. When they met, out back where the priest had his stone house, Father Ordoñez was tending a meagre lot of chickens. The priest was, in Juan Valdez's new view, a humourless, juiceless, man; the kind that had most certainly to bring more anguish to the Little Jesus than he brought comfort.

Father Ordoñez closed the gate upon his chickens and said, 'Good evening, Juan. Maria probably explained, did she not, about the American?'

'She explained,' echoed Juan Valdez. 'If he will be satisfied to see the old watchtower and perhaps the stone ruins of that aqueduct, Father, I will be pleased to show them to him. Of course.'

The priest did not smile, showed in fact no gratitude at all, probably because, having dedicated a whole lifetime to doing things he had never especially wanted to do, he could see no reason to thank someone else for being this way merely one time.

'Well then, Juan, you may care to go down to Holquin's inn this evening and introduce yourself. I have already spoken to the American—whose name by the way is Herbert Smith from Nebraska, U.S.A. I told him this afternoon when we met as he was returning from a tramp in the westerly hills that you would come see him, if it were agreeable that you would do this thing.' Father Ordoñez raised grey eyes made as dark as wet steel by the night. There was no appeal, no gratitude, and no compromise in them, and although he clearly expected an answer, he had not really asked a question as much as he had given an order.

Juan repeated the name with a thin hope rising within him. 'Herbert Smith of Nebraska, U.S.A.'

The priest's brows drew inward just a little,

showing impatience at what he probably assumed was stolidity. 'You only have to use the name, Herbert Smith. *Señor* Smith. The other is simply where *Señor* Smith derives from. You do comprehend?'

Juan nodded, clinging to his thin hope. 'I understand, Father. I will go arrange with *Señor* Smith for the little walk tomorrow.'

'Excellent, Juan. And remember; *Señor* Smith is not as young as are you, and most probably of an inferior physical capability, so you will be tranquil with him.'

Juan again nodded, and turned to depart. Father Ordoñez watched him shuffle from sight around the near side of the church, and wanly shook his head. Then he went to be certain the gate was firmly latched upon his chickens. The salary of a parish priest, as the Good, Sweet Lord knew, was meagre enough, but with eggs and meat from his little flock, and milk and cheese from the parishioners, well, in even a stagnant back-water such as Villa Real had of necessity to be, a frugal man could manage well enough.

Juan Valdez paused out front in the woolly night gazing in the direction of Pablo Holquin's building. The weaker segment of him shrank back but the stronger part was persuasive. It was not dominant; that forcefulness had begun to atrophy almost after the first awakening that first day upon the mountainside. It was persuasive with a quite

193

strength derived from a dread of loss. All Charles Southcott wanted was to be left alone until he could lose himself entirely in Juan Valdez. This was the only way he could conceive of being able to complete the total settling-in.

He stepped forth with reluctance, but at least he stepped forth, heading slightly downhill toward the inn. An old she-goat, who undoubtedly had escaped from someone's pen bleated of her plight, and Juan Valdez who normally would have searched out her home and returned her to it, simply looked at her and kept walking.

It was past dinnertime. Most of the houses had a light or two although some were already dark. People rarely went strolling; the older ones, although they would have denied it to the death, never went more than a few yards from their cottages after night fell because locked in their secret hearts were the uneasy afflictions of earlier times when people knew positively that devils skulked close by after the sun left and before the moon rose, wrenching out souls to whisk away to Hell.

One person, a stocky man, leaned out front of Holquin's establishment, and as Juan Valdez padded close this man turned slightly and lifted a face that reflected orange light from within, heightening the angles and shadowing the planes.

Doctor Walter Whalen!

194

The ache in the breast of Juan Valdez turned to a steel hoop around his heart. He halted and impassively introduced himself.

'Herbert Smith' was interested and seemingly pleased. He offered a hand which Juan Valdez had to force himself to grasp momentarily then release. '*Señor* Smith' knew a dozen or more very simple words. In a context that was interesting because it barely expressed a thought in garbled continuity, he agreed to be at Juan Valdez's cottage a little past sunrise. He would, he said, ride his motor-bike up that far and if Juan Valdez did not object, he would leave the motor-bike there, so it would be available for him to ride back when they returned.

Juan Valdez did not object at all. He studied the face of Doctor Whalen, which seemed leaner and more worn now than he remembered it, although he decided this might not be true because the Southcott recollections were not nearly as strong as they had once been, a week or two earlier.

Walter Whalen may have sensed something; perhaps he thought this young shepherd was trying to arrive at some private assessment of him, but at any rate he smiled and made a little hand-gesture. In a perfect sentence, learned entirely by rote from Pablo Holquin, he said that it was indeed a beautiful night.

Juan Valdez pulled himself round and glanced from the clear heavens to the farther-out drop-away of countryside. 'Yes, Mister,' he agreed, 'it is indeed a beautiful night. Now I must return. I will await you in the morning. Good night, Mister.'

Walter Whalen smiled and inclined his head, and continued to lean where he was until long after Juan Valdez had passed from sight in the uphill gloom; until even the soft sound of his cadenced footfalls faded and were lost.

Perhaps tramping an upland pasturage with a handsome young shepherd of Catalonia would not put him closer to his objective, and then again perhaps it might. If anyone would know which were the most beautiful women of Villa Real it would be a *young* man. One thing was a fact; Walter Whalen could hardly barge up to some stranger and ask about the beautiful women of Villa Real. And even more inexcusable would be any such discussion with that hatchet-faced priest.

The night remained bland and clear, promising that the day to come next would be equally as pleasant, and after Juan Valdez had gone back up towards his home and his Maria, and long after Walter Whalen had ambled on through to his bedroom at the back of Pablo Holquin's inn, that lost she-goat kept wandering in and out of places plaintively bleating until an old man who was a light sleeper—Emilio Sanchez—came padding forth to scrutinise her closely, then go rummaging in his hovel for a string to be put

196

round her neck while he led her home. He might at times be vague about which children belonged to which household and family, but he knew all the goats and a good many of the sheep and dogs of his village.

CHAPTER TWENTY-ONE

'THIS—MUST BE—JUSTICE'

Walter Whalen arrived on his motor-bike, making the village resound to its unpleasant sound, and because it was not the custom in rural Catalonia for the women to interfere in men's business, Maria peeked out at the American, not very interested but very curious, and watched him greet her husband, then fall in with Juan as the flock streamed from the corral to start its daily climb to the mountainside.

For Juan Valdez this was the easiest part. He understood the American even when he stumbled in Spanish, swore in English, and tried a garbled conglomeration of simple words in both languages. To help a little, Juan would point to objects and pronounce a word; *chiva* for the goat nearest Walter Whalen, to the nearest sheep, *borra*, meaning it was a young ewe, to the nearest lamb, *borrego*, and to himself *borreguero*, a shepherd.

197

They spent over an hour walking behind the flock with Juan Valdez pointing to objects such as trees and stones, the higher headlands—*barrancas*—to clouds and different kinds of grass, naming them slowly and listening when Doctor Whalen pronounced their names. When they finally reached an upper level and the flock began to browse, to disperse among the wiry sedge and throughout the little defiles, Juan turned and raised an arm without speaking. At his side Doctor Whalen turned, looked out over the magnificent landfall with Villa Real small and clustered and picturesque in its ancient setting, and said, 'Beautiful.' He spoke in English. 'So peaceful.'

Juan turned to lead off along a faint indentation that skirted round a low hillock. The trail was obviously quite old but it did not look as though it had been used much in a long while. Below a serrated high bluff where there had once been a living spring, one which had probably run a considerable head of water, there was now little more than a half acre of marsh-grass, some trees of considerable height and girth, and the tiny tracks of small animals who came to this place to eat green grass.

Here, there was the beginning of a stone causeway, and upon its upper level there was a mortared stone flume which commenced about where that ancient spring had been, then ran outward and downward perhaps a hundred

198

yards, and ended.

Walter Whalen was impressed. He climbed to the causeway's top and inspected the ancient stone masonry. Juan remained below with his gaze fixed almost fiercely upon the little square of stone far away where Maria was, where his olive trees and his stone pen looked so small in the quiet light of mid-morning.

Whalen called down. 'Who built this thing?'

Juan did not glance up as he replied. 'Who knows, Mister? It is said the Romans started it. It is also said that as soon as they dug deeper to increase the water's flow, they disturbed the water spirit, and he made the water dwindle away.'

Walter clambered back down and dusted his hands. He shook his head. 'A thousand years ago, perhaps. Maybe even more.'

Juan smiled and turned to walk on past the ruin. There was a stone tower beyond the big trees which was not visible from the village. It had somehow managed to stand without much serious deterioration since about the time the viaduct had been begun. The trail leading to it was equally as vague as the trail had been to the marshy place.

The tower had undoubtedly been erected for the purpose of keeping watch from the highlands, towards the seacoast where Rome's enemies would arrive by ship.

Walter Whalen stopped when he saw the tower and leaned back to see its top. 'Sixty feet, at least,' he said in English. Juan smiled and led onward.

At the base of the tower underbrush was thick and wiry as heather grew to the height of a man's waist. Foraging goats and sheep had left bits of their hair upon the native growth where they had chewed their way through to create pathways.

At one time there had undoubtedly been a stout oaken door but now there was simply the narrow opening, and beyond that, stones built like steps that protruded from the inside wall with no baluster, nothing to cling to as one climbed to the battlement lookout-stand. It was dark everywhere except directly down the middle of the echoing circular tower; sunlight struck down through from the centre of the stone cat-walk up there, which was where the soldiers had paced, or had simply stood and lounged, while keeping watch.

Juan knew this place well. He took Doctor Whalen inside, showed him the protruding stone steps, and offered to precede him, something Whalen seemed perfectly willing for Juan to do. They started up, and for twenty or thirty feet Walter Whalen had no trouble, but after that for the balance of the climb through the darkness that never left the walls of this stone tower, he groped along the cold, rough wall on his right side feeling for things to grasp. That round shaft of light coming from above showed the stone floor below. It was rather like being suspended in space.

Then they reached the stone cat-walk, and here, at least, those indifferent stair-builders had made a circular stone kerbing completely around the centre hole, where daylight fell through, while in front, looking outward, there were stone battlements at least as high as a man's waist.

It was not hard to imagine why the Romans had put this tower where it stood. The view commanded not only all the lowlands from Villa Real on towards the coast, it also offered a most excellent view of the countryside to the right and left, and out across the blue-grey distant sea.

Juan leaned and looked—not far off, but much closer. But there was no one, no other shepherds, hikers, not even old Emilio Sanchez who came often and robbed building stones from this place, or gathered dead limbs among the great trees. Juan had seen the old man worrying squared building rocks loose from the tower to carry them back down to the place where he had been mending a stone goat pen for years and had not completed it yet.

Walter Whalen admired the view, and when he turned, Juan was leaning calmly, looking at him, his peasant, handsome face calm with resolve. Walter smiled and said, 'Magnificent, is it not?'

Juan looked casually, then looked back and spoke English. 'Why did you have to come?'

Whalen stiffened, stunned and breathless. It hit him so hard he could not find a single word for half a minute. *He remembered that voice!*

Juan waited. He had all day, and even if someone did happen along it was not going to make any difference. He knew exactly what was going to happen.

Walter pushed out a hand to a segment of worn-smooth battlement. 'But—I thought it would be a beautiful girl. Aphrodite in the dust...'

Juan continued to be relaxed and easy, with the pleasant sunwarmth across his back and shoulders. 'That would be my wife, Doctor Whalen, Maria. How did you do it; how did you find out?'

'Your memory-bank went too, along with your psyche, Mister Southcott, God knows no one was more surprised than I was . . . you said something in your sleep one time and your wife remembered it. You said: My God, Aphrodite brought to earth in the dust of Spain. I theorised that you might—that your misplaced psyche might—seek out some particularly appealing memory and settle-in again.'

Juan pondered this. 'Besides Margaret whom did you tell this to?'

'About my theory of where your psyche might be? No one. I didn't dare. And now I'm wanted by the law in Massachusetts. I have a newspaper back at the inn which gives all the lurid details. Mister Southcott, my gawd I've got to find a way to get you back—to get your psyche back.'

Juan ignored the last outburst. 'A fugitive? Well then, I suppose that accounts for the name Herbert Smith.'

Walter nodded. 'It does. It also accounts for my being in no haste to leave Villa Real. I *can't* go back, I can't even let John Ames know where I am, until between us we can somehow devise a way to return you. There are only two people in this world who know what's happened.'

'Only one man, Doctor Whalen.'

'What? What does that mean?'

'I am Juan Valdez. My wife is Maria Peralta Valdez. You saw my house and my flock, and you have been a short while in my village. My life is here, and only here. So—I am not going back.'

Walter Whalen stared, then stepped to the battlement and turned troubled eyes in the direction of the village. After a while he spoke again, quietly.

'There's got to be some way, Mister Southcott. You can't ... what will happen to me, to Doctor Ames, to Boston General? Did you know your wife is suing for five million dollars?'

Juan's eyes showed dark irony. 'God. That's how she'd do it, isn't it? Get more wealth. Doctor, have you any idea what *real* frustration amounts to. Well, no matter.' Juan

203

straightened up. 'I'm sorry, Doctor Whalen. If there were some other way.' Juan moved gently toward Whalen, and as comprehension came, Walter braced for a struggle, then, on the spur of the moment he whipped around, saw the stone steps leading downward upon the opposite side of the tower from which he and Juan Valdez had climbed to the top, and after a wild look back to see how close Juan was, he started desperately downward.

Juan did not hasten at all. He too went to that opposite stairway and as Whalen hastened Juan started downward much more slowly. The tower echoed with their passage. From sixty feet down it would have seemed to someone looking upwards as though there were two men, one in reckless haste, the other one more slow and cautious, flitting downward upon the black-shadowed far wall.

Then Whalen fell headlong from forty feet up. He did not cry out so much as he made a ringing kind of loud gasp that echoed round and round, then dissipated up through the hole where sunlight came down to the floor below, and Juan, stopped, then turned back. From the top, he crossed over and began the descent down the far set of stone steps. Below, lay Walter Whalen like a broken doll in the murky circle of sunlight.

Juan got all the way down and shuffled over to stand above the body. It did not seem that a man could survive a forty-foot solid fall to a stone floor and live. Juan sank to one knee and looked closer.

Walter Whalen's upper body grated from each shallow-drawn breath, and his gaze upward focused upon—not Juan Valdez, because he could only dimly see Charles Southcott. In a whisper he said, 'This—must be—justice.'

He died.

Juan waited a while longer, to be certain, then he said a little prayer in English, remembered from childhood; the only prayer he had said in about thirty years, and the last time he would ever say a prayer in English.

Outside, nothing had changed, at least nothing that Juan Valdez could see, but before he moved from the tower doorway he distinctly heard the soft slap of shoe-leather coming round the hillside from the direction of the old viaduct.

Emilio Sanchez appeared, his patched sailcloth bag slung over one bony old shoulder. Emilio halted in surprise the moment he saw Juan Valdez, then he recovered quickly and came on, calling ahead that he had seen Juan's flock back a mile.

Juan allowed him to reach the doorway, then he said, 'The American fell from the upper heights, Emilio. He is dead in there.'

Old Sanchez's leathery face hardened into an expression of complete shock, for a moment, then he put down his bag and went closer to peer in. Whalen lay exactly as he had landed.

Emilio breathed a rush of soft words. 'Mother of God have mercy.' The old man suddenly straightened up and peered through the interior gloom.

Juan waited, knowing exactly what was passing through the old man's mind. Emilio cried out, eventually. 'But I did not mean for anything like this to happen. I only removed the stones from the one set of steps, Juan. I left the other set untouched.' He turned to look in anguish at the younger man.

Juan was gentle. 'He simply took the wrong way down. It was not your fault, old one. It was no one's fault, really. Except that perhaps hereafter someone ought to stone-up this old place so that others cannot enter. Well; come along. You can help me take the flock back.'

Old Emilio moved like a corpse, like a body whose soul had been plucked away, but he helped with the flock, an instinctive thing for an old man who had spent all his life with small animals, and although he did not speak a single word as they got the goats and sheep lined out, he kept pace with Juan Valdez, and when Juan said, 'I'll go at once and explain this to Father Ordoñez,' the old man nodded his head and moved his lips in a whimpering, silent prayer.

CHAPTER TWENTY-TWO

WHAT SHALL ENDURE

Villa Real reacted with shock, of course, but on the other hand people had been dying in this place for thousands of years and the acceptance of death was easy. It also helped that the gloomy Catholicism of Spain centred round an eventual passing for everyone, dwelling with much ecstatic misery upon this event.

Pablo Holquin went down for the police to Tarragona while Father Ordoñez went back with Juan Valdez and several others to bring out the body.

No one blamed Emilio, but Francisco Ordoñez pursed his lips in disapproval, wondering aloud why the old man had not taken stones from *outside* the tower. Juan replied reasonably that one old man had not the strength, without tools, to so much as loosen the larger exterior stones, and that ended it until, much later the same day Whalen had regrettably fallen to his death, when the police arrived in cars from Tarragona. The captain, a militarily-erect man with a Basque-look to him, echoed Juan's earlier statement.

'That ruin must be stoned-up. Someone else will be injured up there sooner or later. It

should have been stoned-up years ago. As for
the American, well, all that can be done is for
his consul at Barcelona to be notified. They will
want the body and his effects. We did not bring
a van so someone will have to ride his motor-
bike back to the coast.'

The captain was a thorough man. He took
statements from everyone. Emilio Sanchez
shook like a man with a bad fever, until the
burly Basque took pity and patted him upon
the shoulder, saying, 'Fear not, old one, you
were not particularly at fault. Anyway, this
man was a stranger.' As though that last
remark made everything right, the captain
snapped out crisp orders and one policeman
went to consider the German motor-bike while
the others loaded Whalen's remains into one of
the cars, along with the things Pablo Holquin
handed over, and departed back down the
mountainside towards the coast.

Father Ordoñez still wore his disapproving
expression. 'I suppose we have not heard the
end of this affair,' he told the group that stood
like impassive dark statues out front of
Holquin's inn, watching the little red tail-
lamps grow small.

He was quite right, but not in the way he had
meant his remark. Five days later three men
drove into the village from the direction of the
coast. One was an important official of the
police. Another was an import man of the
government, while the third was a minor

208

executive of the American consulate in Barcelona.

They talked to everyone who had known the dead man; mostly, they interrogated Pablo Holquin who had spent more time with the American than anyone else. But their purpose seemed to be interest, not a matter of fixing blame.

Juan Valdez was there, having returned early from the pasturage this particular day, as he had for almost every day since the unfortunate tragedy, so he heard the important police official tell Father Ordoñez that the dead American had not been named Herbert Smith, nor was he from Nebraska. He was from Boston, in Massachusetts, and his name was Doctor Whalen. It had been in the newspapers, including the newspaper found among Doctor Whalen's possessions, that this dead man was a fugitive from American law. He had performed some ungodly and fiendish medical experiment upon one of the most prominent—and rich—American business-men, and then fled with the law hot on his trail.

Father Ordoñez made a little clucking sound, but because he had so little faith in humanity he did not really look very shocked nor outraged.

And that ended it, as far as the villagers were concerned, except for one final event; the government official made arrangements for

Emilio Sanchez to guide a party of public-works labourers to the Roman watchtower to permanently bar access to the thing. It was said that the official had favoured dynamiting the tower but that the man from the consulate in Barcelona had objected, mildly at least, on the grounds that such a structure was of an historic and aesthetic value.

The tower, then, was left standing, but it was eventually closed up, and old Emilio received a little pay for guiding the workers up there. With this windfall he bought a she-goat, the first such animal he had been able to afford in many years.

Maria told Juan it made her want to cry when she saw the old man taking his one she-goat to the pasturage each morning as though he had a flock instead of a solitary animal. And Emilio talked to the goat, intimately, loftily, sometimes slyly and humorously, as though it were a person; as though, perhaps, it was the wife he had put down, behind the church, twenty or thirty years earlier, or maybe as though the she-goat were that daughter who had gone so gayly to the coast, and had never again been heard of.

Juan nodded in sympathetic silence. For a week he had little to say to Maria, or to anyone else. People reasoned that he had to find himself again, after the tragedy; it was only natural for a man to be inward and withdrawn when he had witnessed such a sad thing, had in fact, been the dead man's companion at the awkward moment when he had fallen to his death.

Maria was patient. She knew how to winnow out the gloom, and she also knew that to try and expedite Juan's return to her arms could turn out badly, so she was patient. A woman probably was, as men said, illogical and emotional and unpredictable, but she was also something else: inexplicably and mysteriously wise about some things.

For Juan the days passed and time came in soft layers to mellow recollection of many things. He could lie in tree-shade upon the mountainside with the flock nibbling close by, and let the superimposition of the Southcott psyche complete its engulfing grasp of the Valdez id.

Inevitably peace arrived from the melding, even long before it was complete. There was no reason for Juan Valdez not to know peace. He was doing what his father and grandfather had done before him, as well as his great-grandfather, and, as far as he or anyone else knew, his great-great-grandfather. It was endemic in the Valdez heritage. It provided a living, without luxuries, true, but since childhood the priests had been warning Juan Valdez and everyone else, not just in Villa Real but throughout gloomy rural Spain, to avoid the evils of sensuality, and therefore Juan Valdez was content and at peace.

A man lived, and a man died, and between the first Mass and the Miserere there was a difficult time of pain and small triumph, of some strife, and some struggle, and somewhere between there was a soft time for bequeathing to a woman the whole substance of a man's earthly existence. Subsequently, there was a little more time, then that was all.

Contentment to Juan Valdez was the vision of his village on the twilight trail down from the mountainslope, the sight of Maria Peralta standing full and magnificent and gypsy-like with her great wealth of black hair being stirred by an uphill small wind. It was peace in his heart and serenity in his mind, and a faint stirring of some thrusting power of will, a little blunted by the Valdez heritage, that would ensure that he would always prosper.

When he eventually let go of the other thing and met Maria on a moon-marked bland night out back by the stone pen, she knew he had let go—although she had thought all along it had been something to do with the tragedy—because he slid a strong arm round her middle, the flared fingers flat against her belly, which had as yet not begun to swell, and he said, 'I think the only footprints a man leaves after him are those of his sons,' and dug into her yielding flesh with his fingertips, which made her twist half around and bruise him with her fierceness.

There was the full moon this night, too, but

those old Pagan things were purest superstition. Even if they were not, neither she nor he needed that blazing pale light upon them again. Yet it was up there, and where it touched her face and golden shoulders, and where it brushed across the hollow of her throat leaving a shadow, it brought up the soft paleness of her beauty in a way that sunlight never could.

She pulled him down and whispered of their son, then changed it to sons and clung to him with savage possessiveness while he blocked out the night as well as her beauty by closing his eyes for one last, vivid moment, remembering a cold, heartless face in the austere setting of a house that had never been a home.

That moment passed and he heard a little breeze stir leaves in the olive trees roundabout, and seconds later he was able to wilt at Maria's side unwilling to think of anything but this.

She kept an arm beneath his head while looking steadily upwards where the stars clustered. 'It will all be normal again, from here on,' she murmured. She rallied slightly to add something to that, with a little heat. 'And the next time Father Ordoñez wants someone to be a guide for tourists, let him do it himself or get someone else.'

Juan smiled towards her cameo profile. He flopped onto his back, arms outflung, and also looked upwards. 'Tomorrow you can come up

213

to me on the mountainside with cheese and milk. We can begin to consider names.'

She laughed softly. 'Names? Already? Even sharp-eyed Margarita Holquin hasn't noticed yet. No one knows. Well; excepting Father Ordoñez, no one knows. And what kind of names?'

This was blissfully pleasant. 'Boys' names, of course.'

'All right. From hundreds we can settle upon a boy's name. And what if it is a girl?'

'It can't possibly be a girl,' he stated, and raised a languid arm towards the sky. 'Don't you remember which position the moon was in—that night?'

She rolled her head slightly to see where the moon stood, beyond the fretwork of olive-tree branches. Then she snorted at him. 'You know that isn't so, that old tale. Father Ordoñez wouldn't like even hearing you say such a thing.'

'No; but then I wouldn't be lying here with Father Ordoñez, either.'

'That is disrespectful.' She raised up and propped her head on one palm. 'Aren't you ashamed?'

He smiled. 'Yes, if you wish for me to be.' He touched her. 'You have skin like cool velvet.'

'And you have muscles like steel. And do you know where this kind of talk is going to take us?'

He laughed up at her. 'Not on an empty
214

stomach. You have not given me supper yet.'

She started to move but he caught hold and kept her still. She said, 'Well; how do you expect me to go make your supper if you keep me here?'

'I was teasing, Maria. I'm not hungry.'

'But you haven't eaten since mid-day, so you have to be hungry.'

He thought about that. Maybe, with a woman, it was different. Maybe, once she was settled, she could make an easy transition back to brisk orderliness, but he knew for a fact a man could not do this. He held her there, and when she yielded, he loosened his grip.

'Where do you suppose the American is?' he asked, and she looked shocked before she stammered an answer.

'Well; wherever all the others are. You know, anyway. The priests say they are sleeping, waiting until—'

He rolled his head back and forth. 'No. Maria, I don't think that is the truth.'

She took back a sharp breath. 'Juan!'

He grinned into her widened eyes. 'Is it so terrible, then, for a man to have an occasional thought of his own? Where does it say that Father Ordoñez has to do all my thinking; tell me that, please.'

She struggled to arise again, and this time she was not restrained. He lay there watching her, and when she spoke he was already forgetting what had been said, because to see her erect like that in moonlight was enough to put any man's more sober thoughts to flight.

'Juan; you have changed a little since last year. You even sound a little—I don't know how you sound, exactly, but I know you have changed.' She paused and smiled down at him. 'So have I.' She offered him a hand. 'Come along to the house and be fed ... Juan, I'll tell you something I thought much about today: how is it that all women and I suppose all men as well, who are married and who have had children, could have felt exactly as we do right now, when I am told by my heart that no woman could conceivably ever love a man as I love you?'

He allowed himself to be pulled to his feet. As he stood erect looking down at her, he felt only as Juan Valdez could feel, and yet his mind was clearer, more incisive, than the gentle and ineffectual mind of Juan Valdez actually was.

He took her hand and went slowly back out of the trees and around the stone pen where the flock was bedding down, before he answered.

'I suppose it is because God has willed it to be this way. Why else?'

They reached the rear of the house and some kind of night-bird flew up off the roof. Maria froze in her tracks. Juan watched the bird depart silently, then looked at his wife. So— she did not believe in any of the old superstitions, but that bird had momentarily

216

terrorised her. A black bird rising from one's rooftop on a full moon night. He shrugged, unable to recall if he had ever heard what this might portend.

She loosened, finally, and went past him to enter the house without meeting his glance. He smiled to himself in the moonlight and gave her a hard slap as she went past. Maria squealed and massaged the sore spot, standing very indignantly erect as he came ahead into the kitchen to grope for the light and to get it brought to full brightness.

Across the orange glow that quickened gradually to life, his white teeth flashed in a smile. 'It's all right if other people share this feeling, as long as they never try to take any part of it from us. No?'

She stopped rubbing the sore place and ran over to his arms. As he swept her in close she said, 'Juan Valdez, you are never going to be fed if you do not stop.'

He didn't care. He had already made up his mind, long ago, that this was never going to stop. Not any of it.